CW01095432

ISBN 978-0-484-13663-1
PIBN 10709666

FB &c Ltd, Dalton House, 60 Windsor Avenue, London, SW19 2RR.
Company number 08720141. Registered in England and Wales.

For support please visit www.forgottenbooks.com

CONTENTS.

INTERWEAVING.

CHAPTER I.

STIFLED WITH ROSES.

What shall I do, my friend,
  When you are gone forever?
My heart its eager need will send
  Through the years to find you, never.
And how will it be with you
  In the weary world, I wonder;
Will you love me with a love as true
  When our paths lie far asunder?

MARY CLEMMER.

THE twilight was quite gone. The evening star stood no longer pale and lonely in the heavens, but shone a king of brightness among his fellows. The night was come. The girl in the old-fashioned garden waited still, as she had done since the setting sun had first begun to paint the west with gold and purple, although it was long past the time that Henry Matthewson had appointed in the note a boy had brought her from the village that morning. The dew lay heavy and thick on

TO

Mary Lowe Dickinson,

WHOM AS A WOMAN I HONOR,

AS AN AUTHOR I ADMIRE,

AS A FRIEND I LOVE.

"To-night! O Harry! this very night?"

Every word was a wail; and his tone was tender as he said, "I am sorry, dear, but it must be to-night. Will it be hard to let me go?"

"Hard to let you go!" she exclaimed passionately. "Hard enough, but harder after you are gone. It was dull and wearisome here before you came; but my life had had nothing it might not keep, so I had no sense of missing anything. But now things can never be as they were before. The days will drag themselves along, and the realization of the difference between them and the days that have been will drive me wild. How am I to live through them while they grow into maddening weeks and months?"

If the light had been sufficient, an observer might have seen a smile of gratified vanity playing around Matthewson's lips as he listened. Lightly he answered her,—

"Don't take the matter so to heart, my child. There are partings and meetings every day. No uncommon thing has come to you, little one. Some other man may come this way and find you out as I have done, and help you to while away the time you fear will drag so heavily. I envy him if he does, upon my word."

"If one should come I should not care to know him," she answered sadly. "There is but one Harry in all the world, I fancy."

Something like self-reproach touched him at these words. This child, who knew no better than to show him all her white, honest heart, trusted him so entirely, and he was not, had not been, playing a true part toward her. But she was a child with a child's fancies. Of course her feelings could not be deep or lasting. Thus he reasoned, and his next words were, —

"You will soon forget me when I am once away, Ina."

A strange, new thought came to Ina's mind, and lifting her dark eyes to Matthewson's face, she asked, —

"Harry, do you think you will forget *me?*"

"No, Ina," he answered unhesitatingly, "I shall never forget you. What! forget one who has made every spot within miles of us interesting, nay, charming, by her presence? who has been my wood nymph, my fairy of field and forest, my star of evening, my everything pure, sweet, and beautiful! I shall always look back upon this summer as the most delightful season of my life, and ever thank you for having made it so."

"And I shall see you again? I shall sometimes hear from you?" Ina asked eagerly, clinging desperately to her faith in him, her eyes on the shaded face she could not see.

One more sentence and her faith and hope were gone.

"The world is wide, dear," he said. "Who can tell whether we shall meet again? I certainly hope we shall. Another summer may find me here as the last has done. I am so poor a correspondent I won't ask you to write me, for you would probably not receive fair replies to what I feel would be charming letters."

Long he lingered in the night-enshrouded garden saying those pretty, meaningless things which men are saying to women every day, thinking, perhaps, to atone in part by a thousand flatteries for one enormous sin. As Ina listened, a passage from the English history she was reading with her uncle Mark came to her mind. Disraeli speaking of the high compliments paid to Sir Walter Raleigh by those who went to inform him of his coming execution, said, —

"It was stifling him with roses."

This was the sentence Ina recalled as Matthewson talked. He left a light kiss on the hand he held in parting, and said as he turned away, —

"Good-by, my friend of a summer, good-by; don't forget me."

She did not know what answer she made. A feeling of desolation swept over her, and she realized that she was alone with the night and the stars and her ruined faith.

"And this is all," she said wearily. "I am what he called me, his friend of a summer — nothing more. And in other summers he will have other friends, and I shall be forgotten, or only remembered as a plaything without which the hours must have passed too slowly. Oh! what a bright, brief, glorious, dangerous season this has been!"

CHAPTER II.

GLANCES BEHIND.

I could paint you his quaint, old-fashioned house
  With its windows square and small,
And the seams of clay running every way
  Between the stones o' the wall.

ALICE CARY.

The human race are sons of Sorrow born,
And each must have his portion.

THOMSON.

ONE bright spring morning, forty-seven years before our story opens, a young man and a fair girl stood before their pastor in the village church in which they had worshipped since their earliest recollection, and spoke the words which bound them together for life. To the farm, with its large old-fashioned buildings, which his father had bequeathed him, John Winter took his bride, and a new home was formed; not merely an abiding place, but such a home as loyal, loving, patient hearts and willing hands alone can make.

When one year, a glad, busy year, had gone by

there appeared a little stranger in the Winter household; a dainty morsel of babyhood, with its father's dark hair and its mother's regular features, and clear blue eyes. In the beautiful month of May the baby came, and May her name became.

As time went on other children came until six were born. Healthy, happy children they were, and their parents looked forward to a time when their old age should be surrounded and protected by those of their own household.

But before May had completed her tenth year, an epidemic swept through the neighborhood, and when the next winter's snow fell it covered four small graves, and on four tiny headstones the name of Winter was carved. May, the eldest, and Mark, the youngest of their children, were all that were left to the stricken parents.

It was a time of severe trial at the farm. The mother's heart seemed broken, and the father, tender as strong, who had loved his little ones so dearly, grieved as sorely for his wife's sorrow as for the loss of those who had gone to live other lives in another world.

But spring came with its lessons of hope, and

the grass grew soft and green above those four short graves, and submission, and later peace, came to the mourning ones.

Quietly the years stole away, with no special events to mark their course, and John and Sarah Winter began dimly to realize that May was a young lady, and that baby Mark was fast outgrowing jackets and his first arithmetic.

One day it came to the knowledge of her parents that May had a lover. I think all fathers and mothers rather dread the appearance of their daughter's first lover. It gives them pain to know that their darling finds any love sweeter and dearer than the home love. And then May's lover was certainly not wholly unexceptionable. Not that his habits were bad. Indeed, it might almost be said that he had no habits. He was everything and nothing. To-day an artist, to-morrow a newspaper correspondent, the next making plans for drawing a fortune from some mine, and again hiring out with some farmer to till the ground. While on a visit to a relative who lived near the Winters, he met May, and immediately a strong affection sprang up between the two. Hugh Ellerton was very handsome, with a dark, rich beauty inherited from a Spanish grandmother, very fascinating with his perfect manner and intelligent conversation. No wonder May's heart was taken by storm. In three weeks from the time of their first meeting Ellerton had asked and obtained her consent to be his wife. The parents were told of the promise asked and given, and at once set about trying to learn something of their daughter's lover. The relative at whose house the young man was staying said that "Hugh was a good enough fellow, only there was no stability to him. Couldn't stay in one place more'n six weeks at a time," and that he "had no one to depent on, for all his near relation was dead."

Not a brilliant outlook for their daughter, thought prudent John Winter and his careful wife, and both tried earnestly to persuade May to break her hastily formed engagement, but in vain. Usually so obedient and easily entreated, she was obstinate in this matter, and at last a reluctant consent was given to her marriage. Hugh Ellerton, with his usual impetuosity, urged an immediate union, and again the village church was the scene of a wedding, and the same minister, now grown old and gray, who had married John and

Sarah Winter, performed the marriage ceremony for their daughter and her chosen one. And again, when two years of May's married life had passed away, there was a baby girl in the Winter home. The young people had stayed at the farm; for John Winter objected to his daughter's leaving it, and Hugh, who had no home to which to take her, loved her too well to leave her. The child was named Ina two days after her birth, and the next day after her christening the young mother died. There was a longer grave made by the side of those already in the churchyard, and of the six children she had borne but one was left to Sarah Winter.

Hugh Ellerton could not be comforted, and in desperation fled from the place where he had spent the happiest and unhappiest days of his life. For a year the Winters heard occasionally from him; but at last his letters, never dated twice from the same place, ceased altogether. And the child Ina grew from babyhood to girlhood with only such knowledge of her passionate, ne'er-do-well father and the sweet young mother who had died so soon after her birth, as was imparted to her by others. From her father she inherited her clear, dark complexion, her wavy hair, and large, deep, lustrous eyes, and her passion and sensitiveness of soul; from the Winters her scorn of falsehood, her abhorrence of all unjust dealings, her energy of character.

To this child, who had been given them in the autumn of their lives, John and Sarah Winter, as well as their son, gave the tenderest love, the most unselfish care. She obtained the best education which the district and village high schools could afford. She learned rapidly and remembered well. At fifteen she left school, and after that read much alone and with her uncle Mark who was eleven years her senior.

I suppose all maidens dream dreams; and Ina's were of the most romantic sort. Walter Scott's novels were her delight, and the adventures of King Arthur and Galahad interested her far more than the right ways of doing household work or of caring for household linen. She was often a puzzle, sometimes a discouragement, to Grandma Winter, who, like all thrifty New England housekeepers, thought girls should first of all learn how to do domestic work well. But Mark said comfortingly, "Never mind, little mother, Ina will find her work and do it well. We are not all born to the same things."

When Ina was seventeen a change came to her life. Henry Matthewson came to spend a few weeks at the village inn whose keeper was his uncle.

The people of country towns are not long in finding out all that can be learned concerning a stranger in their midst, and it was asserted that Matthewson was rather a fast youth.

The report that his father was immensely wealthy was not doubted, for the gentleman arrayed himself in the most costly and becoming manner, and a small beautiful diamond gleamed in his shirt front.

Ina met the young man at some rural gathering, and at once became the object of his devoted attention. He found her handsome where other girls were plain, fresh and more interesting than most girls he had met, and blessed his stars that some one had been found to help him pass more swiftly the long, listless country hours. He had read her favorite books, he could recite with great effect her favorite poems. He knew she admired him, that he had become her hero, and sometimes caught himself wishing that he was all she thought him. But he was what circumstances had made him, and it was too much trouble to make one's self over. He would take the good the gods provided — why not? — and have a pleasant and idyllic summer. Thus he reasoned with himself. There was much rural gayety that season. Picnics, rows on the lake, tennis, — this last game introduced by Matthewson, — excursions after wild flowers and berries, and Ina saw much of her new friend. Her grandparents had heard the reports concerning him, and requested Ina not to become intimate with him, and she really intended to obey them, but he managed to meet her again and again. She became entranced, intoxicated, bewildered, and believed no ill report of her prince could be true, and that her grandparents were misinformed. You know how it ended. I have told you of that parting in the garden. The sweet, false words were all said, her friend and her summer were gone, and who shall describe her feelings as she stood alone with the night and the stars and her first pitiful sense of degradation? She was impatient of the great pain at her heart. What had she done that such misery should come to her?

Was her disobedience worthy of such punishment as *this?*

"The world is *false, false!*" she cried, making the mistake we all make at times of judging the world by one person. Before to-night she had been ready to declare all men true because those she knew were so. Now the whole world had become false because one lacked truth. To us who are not sages or philosophers the person whose life touches ours at the nearest point is the one by whom we measure the universe. She had seen the clay feet of her idol. Her dream of a summer was ended. It was midnight when she crept into the house and to her room. She did not know that she was shivering, and that her teeth were chattering as though with ague. Outward discomfort was unheeded before the great, sudden mental trouble that had overtaken her. As she combed out her long hair, she caught sight in the mirror opposite of her pale face, and looking into the great, burning, reflected eyes, she said slowly, sadly, —

"My childhood has gone from me, and it is a *terrible* thing to be a woman!"

CHAPTER III.

MADGE.—NEW PLANS.

I feel a newer life in every gale;
  The winds that fan the flowers,
And with their welcome breathings fill the sail,
  Tell of serener hours —
Of hours that glide unfelt away
Beneath the skies of May.

PERCIVAL.

And such a want-wit sadness makes of me
That I have much ado to know myself.

SHAKESPEARE.

A TRUE "son of the soil" was Mark Winter, tall, bronzed, broad of shoulder, sinewy of limb; a farmer because he chose to be so, but no clodhopper; a lover of good books, a shrewd observer of men and things, a kind son to his father, a tender one to his mother, careful of those of his own household and of all creatures over whom he had charge; silent for the most part, for words did not come easily to him.

It was the month when roses blow, on a clear bright morning, that we introduce him to you.

He stood with his hat in his hand, the breeze playing with his dark hair, his face towards the east watching the sun come up. Every clear morning for years, except on those rare ones when he had been prevented by illness, he had watched and waited for the sunrise, but his hazel eyes softened on that June day as though it was some new sight he beheld. He was in accord with the morning, and nature spoke to him as she only does to those who understand and love her. When the sun was fairly risen, he turned again to his occupation, which was fastening a rosebush to a trellis which he had made in some of the odds and ends of time which came into his busy life. When the work was finished he plucked a half-blown rose from the bush, saying under his breath, "So like her cheeks. She will like it, I know."

Entering the house he placed the rose beside a plate on the breakfast table. Near the same plate was a fresh napkin, encircled by a handsome ring, and on this ring was engraved the name "Madge." Half an hour later, Madge Munroe found the lovely blossom, and exclaimed as she took it in her hand, "Isn't this beautiful?" never dreaming that the donor had compared it to her own pink cheeks. Those cheeks had been pale enough two months before; so pale, and their owner so languid, that she had consulted a physician, and had been strongly advised by him to leave her boarding-house in the large village, which, with its stores and shops and large manufacturing places, was so like a city, and obtain some quiet home in the real country where she could breathe air unmixed with dust and smoke, and have plenty of fresh eggs and new milk. But to explain how Madge came to be a member of the Winter household we must go back some months in our story.

After the night on which Henry Matthewson bade her good-by, there came many days in which Ina Ellerton lay in a darkened room, burning, shivering, moaning with pain, talking in a way no one understood. Lung fever was the result of a heavy cold taken on the evening when she lost her girlhood.

The doctor's old black horse and well-known sulky stood often and long before the gate of the Winters' front yard, while the physician studied a case in which he felt an uncommon interest, for bright-eyed Ina was an immense favorite with him as her mother had been before her. Grandma Winter hovered about the bedside, carefully administering the exact quantity of medicine at precisely the right time, bathing the hot head, shaking up the tumbled pillows, replying as best she might to the wild questions that no one could answer intelligently. John and Mark Winter came often to the sick-room door, anxious to do all that might be done for patient and nurse. There were days when the doctor came twice or thrice, and on which the entire Winter household put aside ordinary work and waited, fearing, hoping, praying. And after this a blessed moment, when in tones trembling with thankfulness the physician said, "She is better; she will live."

When the last of September came Ina was able to sit up in the comfortable chair which Mark brought from the village furniture rooms for her especial use. In October she was so far recovered that she could go out and wander about the farm, or sit in the autumn sunshine. There was a bench placed beside the summer-house in the garden, and on this she would sit for hours, her head leaning against the building behind her, her thin white hands motionless in her lap, her dark eyes gazing into the hazy distance with a sad, unseeing look in them. While her weakness lasted, life seemed to stand still with her. She had no plans, no hopes, no fears. She only wanted to be alone, and to rest. But as her strength returned, a sort of frantic restlessness took possession of her. She could only work or read for a few moments at a time. When it was morning she wished for night, and when night was come she longed for morning. The days, so full of memories, brought torment; the night, so rife with dreams, witnessed bitter awakenings, and in her young heart she cried out, as many other and older people have done, that there was no sorrow like unto *this* sorrow. Wandering one day in the bright-hued forests, scarcely noticing the beauty that a year before would have made her wild with admiration, new and sudden thoughts came to her, and she sat down amidst the brown leaves which had already come to their perfection and fallen, and communed long and seriously with herself. That night she went to the library where Mark Winter was sitting, and standing before him asked with simple directness if he would arrange for her to learn telegraphy. Mark drew her down on his knee and laid her head on his shoulder before he answered her.

"Tell me all about it, dear," he said. "What makes you want me to make such an arrangement?"

He was not surprised at her request. He had been watching her for weeks, and he knew this was no child preferring a childish and impulsive request, but a woman asking a favor for a woman's reason. But he wished she would talk freely with him, and then perhaps he could better help and advise her. And Ina looked into the grave, tender face above her own, and decided to do what her uncle had asked; to "tell him all about it." The large hand never ceased to stroke her hair as she told of her disobedience and its consequences. Very tightly the hand on Mark's right knee was shut, very firmly the lips beneath the thick mustache were compressed as the low, girlish voice spoke of the persuasions and honeyed words that had been brought to bear upon the summer friend, but not once was Ina interrupted. But over and over again Mark, the silent, was saying to his stormy heart, "'Vengeance is *mine*, *I* will repay, saith the Lord.'"

When the story was finished, the dark, appealing eyes were once more raised to the hazel ones before whose gaze they had drooped, and Ina straightened herself to a sitting posture as she said,—

"Upbraid me, uncle Mark, if you will. I deserve it. But O Markie! help me about the telegraphy. I thought it all out as I sat on the leaves in the wood. I think there must be a *special* thing for each of us to do. I am beginning to understand about the talents. And, Markie, I have something to tell the girls of this world. I can't tell it rightly here. I don't know enough of life. I want to learn telegraphy so I can go away, go into the world and learn to deliver my message."

Again the young head was drawn down to Mark's shoulder, and he said,—

"I will see Miss Munroe to-morrow, and try to arrange for you to receive lessons in telegraphy. And, Ina, we must ask the Father about your case."

And so it came about that Madge Munroe, the village telegraph operator, received Ina as a pupil.

Ina practised with marvellous zest, and her progress was such as to astonish and delight her teacher. She spoke little, but worked unceasingly. All through the winter months she never flagged or wearied, and before the spring came every sound of the relay had a clear meaning to her; and when, through the instrumentality of Miss Munroe, a good position was offered her, she was quite competent to fill it, and begged that she might be allowed to accept it. The situation offered was in another State, and at first John and Sarah Winter strenuously opposed their child's acceptance of it; but Mark, whose good judgment they never doubted, said to them,—

"I believe it is best for Ina to go. She is a woman, and needs interests and employment different from those she has enjoyed as a child. She can resign the office if it is not suitable for her."

And so the matter was settled, and Ina went away, with many tears to be sure, but glad to see new people, and faces that might help to drive from her mind *one* face.

Twice while Ina was her pupil had Madge Munroe accepted an invitation to visit the Winter homestead; and when, a month after Ina's departure, her declining health caused her to seek a physician's advice, and the physician had so strongly advised real country living for the summer, her thoughts turned with a feeling of strong desire to the old farmhouse with its large, sweet rooms and homelike look, and, most of all, its pleasant-faced mistress. When she proffered the request that she might be allowed to make for a few months her home with the Winters, her pale face pleaded more eloquently than her words, and she was at once adopted into the family as one of its members.

A very pretty girl it was that sipped Mrs. Winter's rich coffee, and smelt the lovely rose on that June morning. About the medium height, with a good figure and perfectly fitting garments; her complexion a pure white and pink; her light hair fell gracefully over and half concealed her broad forehead; her eyes were blue, changeful, beautiful; her mouth firm but never sullen;

her manner a blending of dignity and sweetness that was charming,—what wonder that Mark Winter, who never paid her a compliment that any one heard, thought her in his heart a queen among women?

CHAPTER IV.

THE MUNROES.

I could lie down like a tired child,
And weep away the life of care .
Which I have borne, and yet must bear.

SHELLEY.

ON a large farm in the State of New York lived Joseph Munroe with his wife and eight children. His family was a band of laborers. If any of the wives or daughters of farmers read my story they will readily understand why the work in that farmhouse was never quite done, and why all its inmates seemed to be always tired. The Madge of our story was the youngest girl in the family; and in looking back in after years upon her childhood there always arose a vision of the pale, worried-looking face of the mother who was continually trying to make one dollar do the work of two, and whose eyes had in them such a half-frightened look as she told the man whose brow so often clouded at her words, that flour barrel or sugar firkin was empty, or that wearing apparel was needed. She remembered, too, how often there had been disappointed young countenances because something "the other boys all have," or that "the rest of the girls have all got," was denied.

Joseph Munroe was not a bad-hearted man, but one whose hand-to-hand fight with poverty had embittered his soul.

There was no money to buy the books that all would have enjoyed, nothing wherewith to pay for the musical instrument that all desired, and no time in which to read, and study music, had books and instrument been obtainable. The farm and household drudgery went on week after week and month after month with little to make it lighter or easier. Is it a wonder that Madge grew to hate poverty and long for wealth? that in her ignorance she fancied that money would open every door that led to all the joys and pleasures of life?

The years went on until Madge was thirteen. During these years Elizabeth, — somehow the name was never shortened to Lizzie or Beth, — the oldest girl, married, and Amy, the next oldest, left home to become a telegraph operator in a distant State. One of the four boys had died. Three boys and two girls remained at the farm. When Josie was fifteen, and Madge two years younger, the tired mother folded her hands, poor weary hands that had in life found so little time in which to be idle, and rested from her labors; and the two girls became housekeepers; for Mr. Munroe was as little able as ever to hire assistance either in the house or on the farm. What hard, wearisome tasks those girlish hands were obliged to perform in the months that followed! But though the young shoulders drooped the youthful hearts did not wholly fail; and the two toilers talked much of a future that was sure to bring brighter and happier days. A year after the mother's death the father was called away from earth, and the Munroe children were orphans. For a few months George, the eldest son, managed affairs on the farm, and things went on much as usual. But it was a lonely, unsatisfactory life those children led with no wise head to direct, and no strong hand to lighten their labors; and at last they decided to give the old place up to Elizabeth's husband. who was a poor farmer, and each go forth to seek a place in life. In the mean time Amy had been making many new friends, and when the old home was broken up she obtained, through those friends, situations for her brothers, and took both Josie and Madge into her office to fit them for offices of their own. Fortunately for the two girls a new branch of the road on which Amy was employed was completed during their pupilage, and very soon telegraph offices were opened on this branch, and positions were soon obtained for them both.

The natural affection existing between Josie and Madge was mightily strengthened during that time when, while still under the burden of grief for their parents' loss, they labored alone in the old farmhouse, and the love they bore each other was something beautiful. Many hours when their hands were busy with household work did they plan for the future. In the coming time, when they could "go away and earn some money like sister Amy," they would build a house, and make a home for the entire family. The house was to be a thing of beauty in itself, and was to be furnished with soft carpets, beautiful curtains, rich furniture, a grand piano, books, music, everything that would cause its inmates to forget the hard, relentless poverty that had darkened their early lives. These girls were not mercenary; they simply hated poverty because it seemed to them to have caused every woe of their lives, and longed for wealth that the too heavy burdens of life might be eased. In after life, when they learned how hard a thing it is to save money from a moderate salary, their bright dream was not forgotten, or their purpose given up.

It was when Madge had been a telegraph operator about three years that she was offered the position of manager of Brentwood office. As the change would give her a salary nearly twice as large as the one she was then receiving, the position was accepted. She had been in Brentwood nearly two years when she received Ina Ellerton as a pupil.

CHAPTER V.

A PROPOSAL.

I fling my heart into your lap
Without a word of pleading.

WHITTIER.

THE long, sunny summer days formed themselves into weeks and months. June, with its roses and the deliciousness which seems almost too much; July, with its burning noons and pleasant evenings; August, with its weary hours and few breezes, came and passed, and Madge Munroe was still amidst the pleasantness at the farm. The sparkle came into her eyes and lingered there. The pink of her lips became cherry, her limbs regained their former strength. The world was kind, and she was happy. She usually walked to her office in the morning, but often when her hour for closing came she found the gray horse and light wagon from the farm waiting at the door of the station to take her home. Mark was usually driver, and often a circuitous route to the farm was taken and a pleasant ride enjoyed while the night came softly down and the dew fell.

The promise that all things shall be made new was fulfilled for Mark Winter that summer. He had always loved the summer, but surely she had never shown herself so riotously beautiful as now. The flowers, from the modest buttercup to the royal rose, had always been his friends; but somehow they had made themselves far more lovely than was their wont on this season of seasons, and he admired them as he had never done before. The mountains in the distance had talked to him since he was a child; but he had never felt their mightiness as now, or thought them half so grand and brave looking. The sky had always smiled on him, but this remarkable season it had a habit of looking softer and bluer than in the summers gone.

"No wonder He pronounced it 'good,'" he would murmur to himself.

O simple Mark! Did you dream that you were happier because the world was more beautiful, and never realize that it was because you were happier that the world was more fair?

How pure and true and high was his love for

the girl who rode beside him in the twilights, who sometimes floated with him in his boat on the river, who seemed so happy in his home! But he would not ask her love in return till she had had time and opportunity to learn all his ways and her own mind. She should have time to know whether she could be happy always with him and his before she must make a decision in regard to the matter. This was how he reasoned in his honest, manly heart.

And so the summer days slipped by, and the beauty of the earth continued to be a marvel to Mark because he had not learned a secret that you and I know. But one day he realized that summer was gone, and welcomed in September, scarcely less beautiful than her departed sister.

One afternoon in this first month of autumn Mr. and Mrs. Winter received an invitation to spend an afternoon and evening with a neighbor. Mrs. Winter hesitated about accepting this invitation on Madge's account, but her son assured her that he could manage the supper; and thus it was that Mark and Madge took their evening meal alone.

Mark set the table as daintily as a woman could

have done, arranged the fire, put the kettle on, and then went for Madge. This evening the most direct route to the farm was taken, and ere long Madge was in the kitchen making tea which was served in the dining-room.

Mark Winter was a good listener, which is a much rarer thing than a good talker. He said little at any time; but his eyes, his smile, his changing countenance, answered one who talked to him, and made the speaker forget for the time being that the interview could scarcely be called a conversation.

And so at the tea-table Madge talked on topics grave and gay, and Mark replied, but with few words.

When the supper was over, and Madge was clearing the table, a silence fell between the two. Madge was wondering if she could arrange to have Josie come to the farm and spend a week or two, and Mark was thinking as he watched his companion how dainty and sweet was the woman he loved, and how glad he should be if she ever belonged here, in his home, for always. When the last dish was put away he led the way to the library. The open fire sent a look of brightness and comfort into every corner of the room. The early autumn night was chilly. As Madge took the seat that Mark drew before the fire for her she said, —

"How cosey and homelike this fire makes everything seem. I wonder that everybody who owns a house does not have in it at least one place where an open fire can be made."

Mark did not seem to notice the last observation. Coming near her, and resting his hand on the back of her chair, he said, —

"Madge, I would like to make things so homelike and attractive that you would be glad to stay here always. I should make a failure of it if I tried to tell you of my love in fine, high-sounding words, but I assure you, dear, that you are precious to me beyond anything in the world. Will you come and live with us, Madge, as my wife?"

It could not have been the heat from the fire that made Madge's face flush so hotly, for a moment later it turned pale. Her heart gave one great bound of joy, and involuntarily she raised her hands and half held them out to him; for he had left her side and was standing in front of her now. But in another instant her heart almost stopped beating, and her hands fell on her lap. Swiftly her mind went back to that early home where the harassed father, the pale-faced mother, and the often overtaxed and disappointed children used to live, and the thought came to her that probably this man was as poor as was her father when her mother married him for love. She thought how care had crowded out love, and want had taken the place of enjoyment, and in her soul she cried out that it must not be, that she must run no risk of helping to make a home as unhappy as her own had been. There arose, too, in her thoughts the picture of the home she and Josie had dreamed and planned about so much. It might yet become, somehow, a reality if she did not yield to this passion which was moving her so strangely. She was still too young to be very practical. The middle-aged or old will hardly dream that anything can be done *somehow*.

She tried to speak a steady refusal, but the only words that came were spoken tremblingly, and yet so earnestly that her hearer could but know that they were meant.

"O Mark, I wish you had not asked me that!"

A look of pain shot into Mark's hazel eyes, and

his large hand went slowly up to his forehead. He tried to speak bravely, but his voice was a little husky as he said, —

"I wish so too, Madge, if it displeases you. I was foolish to think that you could care for a great rough fellow like me."

"There is nothing rough about you," cried Madge quickly. "Oh! please try to understand that there are reasons — that it is not *you* at all, but something quite apart from you, that keeps me from doing as you wish."

"Never mind," he said kindly, pitying her evident distress even as he stood face to face with his bitter disappointment and shattered hope.

"But I *do* mind," she said. "I like you the best of any man I know, and it hurts me terribly to think I must hurt you. But we must be friends, Mark, the very best of friends!"

"Friends, Madge, the very best of friends," he answered; "and if you ever need — or — want me, remember that friends, real ones, are those whom we allow to help us."

"You are good and generous," she answered, "and I thank you with all my heart. Will you excuse me if I go to my room now?"

He gave her his hand as he said good-night, and when she had gone stood looking into the fire till he heard wheels approaching, and then went out, lantern in hand, to send his father into the house and to care for the horse.

Madge, when she had gained her room, sat down by the window and forgot to go to bed. She told herself with bitter regret that she had wounded the manliest and truest heart in the world, and used every argument she could muster to prove that she had done a wise and noble thing in refusing the affection she craved. The moon was far toward the horizon before she laid her head upon her pillow and sank into a troubled sleep.

In the library, too, a vigil was being kept while the moon was going down. Until the large log which had made the fire which Madge had so much admired was a charred and lifeless ember, did Mark Winter sit before the grate. "It seems to me," he said as though speaking to the rioting blaze, "that my life can never be satisfactory without her, but I don't know as we have any promise of being satisfied in this world. Father and mother and Ina are mine to care for, and *she* may need me some time. Please God I'll be ready for a call from her. The good Lord has given me plenty of sunshine in the past, and now I won't rebel because he has thrown a shadow around me that makes everything look black. I won't ask why he has dealt thus with me, but just bide his time to show me the reason."

The strong man knelt by his bedside that night as he had done every night since childhood, yet not a word came from his lips. But do you not believe the Father understood? Do you not think a prayer went up from that room though the silence was unbroken?

CHAPTER VI.

A GIRL LOVER. — REX HILTON.

Is it possible, that on so little acquaintance you should like her? that but seeing you should love her?

He is complete in feature and in mind,
With all good grace to grace a gentleman.
SHAKESPEARE.

"REX HILTON, as sure as you're growing fat and lazy — and there's no doubt about *that* — I'm desperately, overwhelmingly, and irretrievably in love."

"And who," asked Rex, straightening himself up in his easy-chair and looking in rather a sleepy way at his kinswoman, "is the man who can call forth from my usually reticent relative such a profusion of many-syllabled words? Is it the butcher with whom you hold so many confabs, or the old coal-man I saw you talking so earnestly with yesterday? I haven't noticed anything that looked like intimacy in your behavior towards any other gentleman."

"Let it ever be remembered to my credit," replied Bert with a majestic wave of her hand, "that I forgave you your owdaciousness on this occasion when your speech and manner should be meet for one who has been made the recipient of a tender secret! In answer to your inquiry I will say that the object of my passionate regard is no *man*, — bless you, no! — but, in the language of the interesting, but somewhat soft headed Romeo: —

"'In sadness, cousin, I do love a woman.'"

"I always thought you were capable of doing more than most girls," answered Rex.

"Now, my respected relative, I advise you not to try to be sarcastic," declared Bert. "You never make a success of it. When people can do it handsomely I rather enjoy seeing and hearing them at it. There's Judge Davis; his nose turns up as naturally as though it was made to grow that way, and only got turned downward by accident; and I often think when he answers a remark that don't please him, that probably he looks and speaks as Diogenes did when he told Alexander the Great that he could stand out of the light.

But I'll 'ketch holt of my principles,' as Samantha did, and not say anything sharp to you this time."

"Thanks, most lenient of cousins," said Rex. "But I'm waiting to hear the name of her who has enslaved you."

"Well, now, you needn't look as though you thought what I've said is all nonsense. It's always been a mystery to *me* why men always think we women"—and Bert sat bolt upright and looked as dignified as it is possible for one four feet tall, and with a freckled face, short, crisp hair that *will* not be combed out straight, and a pug nose, to do—"should fall in love only with one of their sex. For my part I think it's sensible to love what's most lovable, and girls, for the most part, are much nicer than men."

"I quite agree with your latter remark," said Rex solemnly.

"It's a comfort to have you sensible," replied Bert. "The name of the lady of whom I think by day and dream by night is Ina Ellerton. Isn't that a pretty name? She is the new telegraph operator."

"And does she return your affection?" questioned Rex interestedly.

"Ah! there's the rub," said Bert; "she ignores me utterly. I've tried in all permissible and genteel ways to get on speaking terms with her, but thus far without avail. One morning when I was in the depot and she came out of her office to give the station agent a message, I purposely trod on her toes, and then, with my best bow, apologized, and remarked that it was a pleasant morning; but she just inclined her head, and looked as though she would like to say she didn't care if it was. I overturned the inkstand outside her window at another time, and spoilt one of my best pocket-handkerchiefs mopping up the ink, hoping she would come out and have a social chat over the supposed accident; but she sat as calmly in her office as though spilling ink and wiping it up with one's go-to-meeting handkerchief was a momentary occurrence. I got the stuff all over my face, and came home a blacker and madder, if not a wiser girl. I've sent three telegrams when letters would have done twice as well, and inquired several times for messages when I knew I wouldn't get any, and if I did it would scare me about to death. But my lady utters only ordinary business words. Oh! my heart! my heart!"

And she ran her hand frantically over her left side, exclaiming: "Bless me! where *is* that troublesome organ? I can't seem to find it."

For a moment after she had ceased speaking did Bert gaze into the fire, and her face grew very grave, and the soft light that often made them beautiful stole into her gray eyes. Then she arose, and going to where her companion was sitting, drew a near ottoman to his feet, and sat down upon it. Resting her arms on his knees, and looking earnestly at him, she said,—

"Dear old Rex, I'm like soda-water. You can't come to the real thing in me till the froth is gone. I left Bert over in that low rocker. I'm Bertha now, and I want you to make me a promise. Will you?"

"I think I may venture to say yes," replied Rex with his slow, sunny smile. "I suppose you won't be freakish while you are Bertha."

"Thank you, Rex," she said. "You are the best fellow in the world, as I've often said before. Well, cousin, the face of that girl, Ina Ellerton, haunts me as a beautiful, sad poem always does. It *is* a poem, an unwritten one, itself. Her features are perfect, and I never saw such eyes as hers. They are indescribable. I can't imagine how any one can see them and not vow himself the slave of their owner forever."

"You rave, my dear," said Rex, putting his hand with a caressing motion on the bushy hair.

"Well, she's worth raving about," declared Bert. "No one ever moved me so strangely. When she looks at me I feel as I do when the organ plays something soft and low in church. I'm surely going to be acquainted with her yet."

"I congratulate her," said Rex, "on having secured so true-souled a girl-lover. But about the promise, dear?"

"I'm coming to that," was the reply. "All this is a preface to it. This Ina is not happy. She is astray somehow. Her face is not the index of a quiet mind. I don't believe she's a day older than I, but I feel that she's away beyond me somehow; that she is struggling in some deep water of affliction or worry, while I have never been even in the shallows of trouble. You always understand my rambling talk, Rex, and I think you will gather my meaning from this chaos of words. Cousin, I want you to promise that you will help that girl. She needs such a friend as you would be."

Rex Hilton did not say he did not know her, or understand why he should help her.

This man had since his childhood been helping some one. No large sums had been given by him towards building colleges or giving gifts to rich men; but in garrets where the fire had gone out for want of fuel, in poor homes where food was lacking, in cases where the rent was due and the tenant's purse empty, Rex Hilton's gold was not withheld.

To those in whose hearts patience was needed, or in whose lives love was wanting, he always brought something to help toward making up for what was missing. An old lady once said in speaking of him:—

"He makes me think of the good Book. One never goes to him in the right spirit but he receives help." His look and hand-shake were like a benediction.

"I will not forget your friend," he said simply to Bert, and she was satisfied. She knew what a promise from Rex meant.

In the principal village of the town of Millerville there stood a great, grimy, smoky-looking building, inside of which brawny, sooty men worked over fires that seethed and roared by day, and smouldered by night. Over the large front entrance to this place was the sign, "Hilton & Son's Iron Foundry." Jason Hilton was the head of the firm, and the Rex we have spoken of was the son. The latter at thirty-seven was still unmarried and living at home. Mr. Hilton was the typical business man, keen, prompt, reliable, just, with "no nonsense" about him; his wife a kind-hearted, home-loving woman, devotedly attached to her family. Bertha Hilton was the daughter of a brother of Mr. Jason Hilton. Her parents both dying while she was an infant, she was adopted into her present home. Rex was her playfellow when a child, her confidant and adviser as she grew older. She loved him fondly, trusted him implicitly, enjoyed his company exceedingly. There was enough of mirth in his disposition to make him a congenial companion in her merry moods, and with all that pleased or troubled her she went to him, feeling sure that he would understand and sympathize with her. And she was never disappointed.

She was wont to say, this fun-loving true-hearted girl, that for the greater part of the time she was just Bert, but when a thoughtful fit overtook her she became Bertha.

At the time I introduce her to you, Ina Ellerton had been in Millerville a month. Business for the firm had kept Rex Hilton out of town since her advent, and at the time she was so enthusiastically described by his cousin he had never seen her.

On the next day after the evening when Bert told him of her desire, he sought the telegraph office, and wrote a lengthy message. He was a long time about it. He stopped between the sentences as though wondering what should come next, and looked at the operator as though the sight of her would suggest what should be written. When the message was finally finished and paid for, he turned away muttering, "Bert was right. She is worth raving about."

CHAPTER VII.

A NEW OUTLOOK INTO LIFE.

The Past and the Future are nothing
In the face of the stern to-day.

ADELAIDE PROCTER.

A lesson which I well may heed,
A word of fitness for my need.

WHITTIER.

THE day had been a long, dreary one to Ina Ellerton. The rain had been coming down since early morning in a drizzling, discouraged sort of way that is so much more depressing than a decided downpour. Travellers had been few, and the railroad station in which Ina's office was situated had been, for the time being, nearly deserted. Ina had been in Millerville five weeks, and long, weary weeks they had proved to her. Silence and seclusion, however strongly desired, are not the best tonic for morbid minds, and Ina was morbid to the last degree. Her office duties kept her employed only a part of the time. She had no sewing to do, for Grandma Winter, doing her child a doubtful kindness, had provided her with all the wearing apparel she would need for a year, and she was not one of those who have a liking for fancy work. It was her wish to make no acquaintances. She had written each week to those at the farm. Sarah Winter thought and sometimes cried over her girl's letters; and indeed they were strange letters for one so young to write. Cynical, bitter, sarcastic words were often traced therein, and the simple-minded old lady who read them over and over, trying hard to understand them, and always failing, would lay the written sheets down in her lap, and while she polished her glasses and then held them in her still fingers, would wonder how it was that girls were so different now than when she was young, and if it was the higher education of women, of which so much was being said in the papers and magazines, that put such things into Ina's mind, and if so, if it was as much to be desired as people thought. She spoke of the matter to Mark, and he said thoughtfully, —

"There's a *lower* education as well as a higher for women, — and for us all if we will take it, — but I've been trying to think it all out, and I believe that Ina will be a better and more helpful woman because of the happenings behind her words. God don't bring every man's heritage to him the same way. To some the sunshine of life is enough to make him what he ought to be; to others sorrow must be burned in that worthiness may come out."

Mark spoke as though talking with himself, and his mother was but little less puzzled by his words than by Ina's; she said no more, but kept the matter in her mind to pray over, and wrote homely, comfortable replies to the letters she did not understand.

Ina had thought, still thought, that she had a message to the girls of the world. But how could she tell it? What girl as bright and ignorant of life, as careless of its consequences as she was before that night on which she became a woman, would read words she must write now if she wrote at all? What publisher, indeed, would print such words? Who cared to read of wretchedness? Who would listen to warnings? Never mind. It was well as it was. Let the world, the delusive, hollow, insincere world, learn by experience as she had done. It was not worth caring about. Ever-more and always it was one person who represented the entire world.

On the day of which I have spoken, a spirit of unrest and bitter burning discontent had taken entire possession of her. When not busy at her desk she had tried to read, and to write her weekly letter home; but book and pen were repeatedly put aside with the passage only partially read, the sentence unfinished. Six o'clock came at last, but she was not hungry, and decided not to go to her boarding-place for tea. She arose and stood by the window watching the rain. While standing there she heard a rap on the message window, and on opening it she received a telegram for transmission. It was signed Hilton & Son, and it was Rex Hilton who handed it to her.

"You will greatly oblige me if you will hurry this," he said. "It is important that we hear from Snyder to-night. I will call again in an hour and see if you have received an answer."

Ina turned away with the message in her hand, saying coldly that she would do the best she could with it, and Rex went toward the door, but evidently a new idea came to him, for he went back and sat down in the ladies' room. The telegram was soon sent, and Ina was idle again. Again she went to the window and looked out. It was growing dusk, and the gloom was deepened by the semi-darkness.

The lines of Longfellow's "Rainy Day" came to the mind of the lonely girl; and the words of the first stanzas chimed so exactly with her mood that she repeated them, and with more pathos than she knew.

"The day is cold and dark and dreary;
It rains, and the wind is never weary;
The vine still clings to the mouldering wall,
But with every gust the dead leaves fall,
And the day is dark and dreary.

My life is cold and dark and dreary;
It rains, and the wind is never weary;
My thoughts still cling to the mouldering Past,
But the hopes of years fall thick in the blast,
And the day is dark and dreary."

Here she paused, and in another instant some one whose tones had in them a ring of assurance was repeating the last stanza of the poem.

"Be still, sad heart! and cease repining;
Behind the clouds is the sun still shining;
Thy fate is the common fate of all,
Into each life some rain must fall,
Some days must be dark and dreary."

"You see you did not repeat the last part of your poem, Miss Ellerton," Rex Hilton said, and then, without waiting for an answer, went on, "I like that stanza well, but I like one from 'A Psalm of Life' better.

> 'Trust no Future, howe'er pleasant!
> Let the dead Past bury its dead!
> Act — act in the living Present!
> Heart within and God o'erhead.'

"I beg your pardon," he went on. "Your office-door was ajar, and your message window open, and so I could hear your recitation, and it did not seem right that the most important stanza should go unsaid."

Ina had turned from the window when his voice first reached her. Her first feeling was one of surprise. She had not known that any person was in the ladies' room, and it was seldom that any one spoke to her now except on business. The people about her who had tried to be friendly when she first came among them, found her cold and reticent, and let her alone as she seemed to desire them to do.

A telegraph operator soon makes a reputation for himself among his wire associates; and the one Ina had made was not an enviable one. With her really loving heart and capabilities of pleasing, she was the most disliked of all the operators on the line. Her wired words, when she vouchsafed any, were oftener sharp than otherwise, and after a little while only business words were addressed to her. She seemed to be standing in open hostility to all the world outside her home. It was a false world, but it was never going to deceive her again. Her loneliness was something pitiful; and as Rex Hilton went on saying the lines of the poem and then addressed her, she could not help a feeling of gladness that some one had noticed her words, had thought of her at all. She tried to put the feeling from her, but it lingered.

"I suppose you are Mr. Hilton," she said, trying to speak haughtily, but failing to keep a little tremor out of her voice, "but I do not know why you have spoken to me."

"I will tell you," he answered; "you may not readily forgive me for doing so, but I have, I acknowledge, been watching you for weeks and hoping to get an opportunity to speak with you. You are not happy. I wish most earnestly to help you to become so. You know now why I have spoken to you."

"More hypocrisy!" were the words that formed themselves in Ina's mind, but she looked at the man before her and could not believe them; for as he stood gazing so fairly and honestly into her face he reminded her of Mark Winter. She could not tell why this was so, for he was short of stature, his hair and heavy mustache were fair, his eyes a dark blue, and instead of a farmer's garb he wore a neat suit lately made by a city tailor. She had not yet learned that on the faces of all who serve Him with consecrated hearts and willing hands the Master has set the same sign.

"How do you know I am not happy?" she questioned.

"Your looks and manner, and the words I have heard you repeat to-night, proclaim it," was the answer. "Try to forgive me if I tell you that you are so busy fretting, persistently, *wickedly* fretting over something that happened in the *then* of your life, that you are shamefully neglecting the *now*."

Surely here was plain talk. No sign of flattery in that speech, and Ina was interested in one who talked so oddly and honestly.

"Do you not think," she asked, "that one may neglect the now without shame?"

"Ah, no!" Rex replied emphatically. "I have somewhere read that in Ruskin's study on a massive piece of chalcedony is engraved the word 'TO-DAY,' which is the author's motto. I think we might all adopt this motto with immense profit to ourselves and the world in which we live. We may stretch out our hands and cry as mightily as we will, but we cannot recall one moment of the past. We may try never so hard and we cannot lift the veil that shrouds the future. But the now is absolutely ours, and it is enough. We are too apt to forget that to-days are what yesterdays are made of, and that according to our to-days will our to-morrows be. If we let the things of to-day fill the hours of to-day, put into the present moments just what they should hold, do our *best* now, we shall find ourselves not only 'growing in grace,' but growing in power; in the power that will enable us to keep our thoughts from anything that will worry us to-day or make us anxious about to-morrow. Mrs. Whitney, speaking from the experiences of a life much longer than yours, says that when we give it all up to God 'he tells us what to do,' and in just doing the one little thing at a time, the thing of the moment,—quite apart it may seem from the great thing of our life we are longing to have justified (adjusted),—we are led toward all the righting and the righteousness. This is the 'justification by faith' which is 'upon all them that believe.' Are you working toward the 'great thing of your life' by doing 'the thing of the moment'? Do you by faith look for the 'righting and the righteousness'? Are you among 'them that believe'?"

"The righting—and the righteousness." She spoke slowly as though to herself, but presently she turned to Rex and said,—

"I was trying to think it out. I have felt there was a great thing in my life to do, and I have looked to myself alone to do it. I have thought I could do the righting, *some* righting at least, and some righteousness would come of it. I have felt goaded on to do this righting, and been worried and tormented by the feeling that my task was set and I was not equal to it. It is a relief to think that after all that some one must stand with or back of me in this work, that not being ready I was not *let* to begin. Perhaps because I had no faith, because I have *not* been among 'them that believe,' no justification—adjusting—has come to me."

She had apparently forgotten Rex again, and looked out steadily at the descending rain as she talked. But again she recalled her thoughts to him, and looking wistfully into his face she said,—

"It is a terrible thing to lose faith in all the world save two or three people. I think I could work and rest if I could trust mankind."

"May I ask," said Rex, "if it is the many or the few who have deceived you? For every one that has been false, have there not a dozen been true? Have you any right to put one against many, and judge the world by a minority? Bear with me a little longer, and let me say that I think there is a great deal of false heroism in the world. Some one wrongs us, and we immediately conceive the thought that the *world* is against us, when our quarrel is not with the world at all. We think it is grand and heroic to distrust all who would make life pleasanter for us, and to stand apart from our fellows as though every one of them had injured us personally. In this way we shut out the sunshine that it is not only our privilege but our duty to accept, and the world generally knows or cares nothing about it. This so-styled heroism is simply foolishness, and is injurious to our happiness, and stands in the way of our mental growth. You are cheating the world far less than yourself, child."

"But something was denied me that I should have had," cried Ina; "something that was my right."

"Denied you by one person, or the world?" said Rex. "And are you sure you were ready to receive the gift, or the gift ready to be given? When the first green fruit appears on the trees, hundreds of little hands are held up for it; but the owners of the hands have no means of digesting green fruit, and the fruit is not ready for any one, and wise parents deny the requests so clamorously made, knowing that by and by there will come to the fruit ripeness, and mellowness, and plenteous pleasant juices, and it will become healthy and satisfying. Perhaps the Father has denied you green fruit, but he has — never doubt it, child — saved for you ripeness, mellowness, rich juices, and pleasant flavors. Live as though you trusted God, and he will show you reasons for things in due season. There will be adjusting, righting, righteousness."

He paused, and Ina said, —

"Go on, please. Talk some more."

"I am glad you wish it," said Rex, "for I want to speak of your work. You feel you have a mission. Work it out earnestly, carefully; but remember the first duty of every one is to *be* the best he possibly can. You may not succeed in painting a great picture, or writing a grand book, or in making your name famous in anything, but you can make of *yourself* all that God has given you material for; and if I mistake not he has given you material for a grand woman, and, if so, you have no right to be anything else. It is the *life* of the painter or the author that gets on to the canvas or the written page. This must be so. Just one thing more. I wish to ask if you ever thought how true is that line: —

'Into each life some rain must fall.'

"Not now and then a life, but *every* life must have its rainy days. But when it is dark we learn to cling more closely to the Father's hand, and he holds a rainbow for every shower."

Ina's signal sounded, and she went to her desk and received the reply Rex expected. As she handed it to him, she said, —

"I thank you for the words you have spoken. I have much to think of, to make up my mind about."

"And I thank you," said Rex, with his peculiarly genial smile, "for listening so patiently. Shall we be friends?" And he held out his hand.

Ina did not reply in words, but she placed her hand in his, and lifted her dark eyes to his face with a look that satisfied him.

When the hour for closing the office came it still rained and the station was deserted, but as Ina went out into the darkness there was a warm feeling in her heart. She *felt* Rex Hilton's manliness and truth, and Rex Hilton was her friend. She found a bright little fire made in her room, and she remembered that once or twice before a fire had been made there when it rained; but it had never occurred to her to be grateful for, or to thank her landlady for this. She would do so in the morning.

It was a pretty and tastily furnished room too. She had not thought of this particularly before. She must be more grateful, more heedful of the "little things of the moment." The righting had begun. By faith, newly awakened, the adjusting of a life had commenced.

CHAPTER VIII.

GOING AWAY FROM THE FARM.

To-night we sit together here. To-morrow night will come . . . ah where?
LORD LYTTON.

MADGE MUNROE remained at the farm till the harvest was gathered in, and the latter part of November came with its short days and frosty nights, and then went back to the village to board. The Winters would have gladly kept her through the cold months, or indeed for any length of time, for she had made for herself a warm place in their hearts, but she wished to go. Never had the subject which had so agitated her on that September night been again alluded too. Mark was just her kind friend, and he had no desire to appear a martyr, but unconsciously to himself the lines about his mouth had become tenser, and a look of endurance had come into his face telling that, however brave and cheerful he might appear, his heart was not untroubled.

"He may forget me if I go away," Madge said to herself, and immediately became far more wretched at the mere thought of his forgetting her. But she felt that it was not best for her to linger in his home.

"In winter trains are often blockaded by snow, and the operator is needed at night to learn of their whereabouts," she told her friends. "It would take so long to come here after me, and for me to get to the station, I am afraid the men would get impatient waiting. And then, you know, it would not be comfortable going through drifts and darkness to the depot."

All this was true, and satisfying enough to two of her listeners; but Madge knew that had all been well between herself and Mark, neither fear of the impatience of any one who might be obliged to wait for her, nor of any discomfort to herself, would have taken her away from the farm.

One cold, gray morning when Mark drove her to the village and left her at her office he took her trunk to her old boarding-place, and returned home feeling lonelier than he had ever felt in his life before.

Early in December came the first snowfall, and

the tall chimneys appeared smokier for the whiteness beneath them, and everything looked exceedingly cold and gloomy to Madge, who, since her departure from the farm, had been wretchedly homesick. The people with whom she boarded were kind-hearted enough, but they were absorbed in their home and children and society affairs, so her loneliness was but little relieved by them. The long weeks of an unusually severe winter dragged themselves along, and every day, with two or three exceptions, seemed so like the one that had preceded it that Madge wondered if anything new would ever happen again. She saw but little of the Winters during the cold season. The old people did not like to go out when the weather was not mild, and the warm days came very seldom that season. Twice during the winter Mark called at her office; once to bring some delicious apples, and again to give her a little bouquet of blossoms that he said his mother had picked from her house-plants for her. He did not add that he had suggested the giving of the flowers, and had himself arranged them in a way he thought would please her. The days on which his calls were made were not like the other days to Madge, and his fruit and flowers were not altogether enjoyed because of their rich flavor, or for their beauty and fragrance.

The monotonous days passed as surely as pleasanter ones could have done, and much-longed-for spring came at last. It found Madge restless and unhappy, and when its months were quite gone, and half of June was past, she was delighted at receiving a request from the superintendent of the company that employed her that she would accept for three months the position of operator at Silver Beach, a small seaside place which was beginning to be exceedingly popular as a summer resort. An unemployed operator was engaged to fill her place, and a letter sent saying she would accept the proffered situation.

Before leaving town she found time to visit the Winters. They had hoped she would again be with them during the summer, and were disappointed that she was going away. But they made the most of her while she stayed, and her brief visit was one to be remembered.

When the nicely prepared supper had been partaken of, and twilight was becoming night, she said good-by to Mr. and Mrs. Winter, and rode to the village with Mark. Her heart was very tender amidst all the tenderness of the young summer, and had Mark renewed the subject of the September before, her answer might have been different from the one spoken on that autumn night. But her manner toward him was not changed, and the few words he spoke were ordinary ones. The ride was a silent one for the most part. The two were each busy with thoughts that might not be uttered. When they reached the gate where they were to part, and Mark had assisted his companion to alight, he held out his hand, and said,—

"I suppose it is to be good-by for a while. Don't forget that you have warm, true friends at the farm, and God bless you—dear!"

I do not think he meant to add that last word, at least aloud, but it had lain in his heart so long, and said itself there so many times, that here, still amid the tenderness of the young summer, it came forth, a fitting word, and he did not attempt to gainsay it, but left her without speaking again.

She stood and watched him ride away, and told herself that no poor man must call her wife; that there was poverty enough in the families of the earth, and yet remembered with a great thrill and heart throb that he had called her *dear*.

Slowly Mark Winter rode home through the moonlight. Old Gray felt the reins lying loosely over his back, and his driver trailed his whip-lash along the roadside, and thought, —

"May the Lord help me to be a man! Whether she loves me or not, I won't, please God, lose her respect."

And the head that was often bared in the sunlight when some inspiring thought came to him, was now uncovered in the moonlight, and the strong face was uplifted, and, as though answering a question, the strong voice said, —

"Ay, Lord, I am biding my time."

CHAPTER IX.

MAKING FRIENDS.

I'll be wise hereafter,
And seek for grace.

Were beauty under twenty locks kept fast,
Yet love breaks through and picks them all at last.
SHAKESPEARE.

MISS MULOCK says, "In most, nay, I think in all lives, is some epoch which, looking back upon, we can perceive has been the turning-point of our existence." In after years Ina Allerton realized that the turning-point of her life was on that rainy night when Rex Hilton spoke so earnestly and plainly to her. A mental reaction took place; the adjusting went on. She learned daily something more of hourly righteousness.

And soon after that memorable talk, or almost monologue, of Rex's, a conversation with that gentleman's cousin helped her greatly. In the early part of one afternoon Bert Hilton stood before the mirror in her room tying and pulling out and retying the ribbon about her neck.

When said ribbon was formed into a bow that she decided was as good as she could make she let her hands fall at her sides, and surveyed herself critically and at length in the glass, and said with a comical grimace, —

"I've always stood to it that my face was just as good and handy to have as any other, if it is a little speckled. And my hair, if not 'a thing of beauty,' has been 'a joy forever,' because it's so little work to care for it. But I must confess that I wish I was a little better looking now, and then perhaps my beauty would notice me without so many strenuous efforts on my part to compel her to do so. Heigho! It's going hard with you, Bert."

On the bureau in front of her was an exquisitely arranged bouquet of carefully selected flowers. An hour had been spent before going to her room in ranging the greenhouse to find blossoms just to her taste.

Donning a light coat and a hat she knew was becoming, she took the nosegay in her hand and walked to the railroad station. She rapped gently on the door of the telegraph office, and when it was opened, without one word of greeting, she held out the flowers, saying appealingly, —

"Please take them. I gathered them for you."

"Oh! how pretty!" cried Ina, and Bert's chains were riveted more firmly than ever, for Ina's voice was as musical as her face was handsome.

"I do not know," Ina said, "whom I am to thank for these lovely things. Will you tell me your name?"

And looking down, the donor softly answered, —

"I am Bert Hilton, and — your girl lover."

With a look of wonder in her eyes, Ina said, —

"I'm afraid I don't quite understand what the last part of your remark means. Won't you come in and explain to me?"

At last her charmer noticed her, and with an ecstatic "Thank you," Bert walked into the office, and in response to Ina's invitation to be seated, drew towards her the tall waste-basket which was about half full of papers, and sat down in it. Her confusion of mind at being received graciously by one with whom she had honestly and heartily, to use her own words, "fallen in love," was so great that I am not sure but she might have sat down on the floor had not the basket been near her, and not realized at all what she was doing.

"Mercy on us! What a sensible party I am, to be sure!" exclaimed she as her feet came up with a jerk nearly opposite her head.

Ina helped her caller from her uncomfortable position, and then the two girls did what perhaps made them feel better acquainted than weeks of ordinary intercourse would have done. Both laughed heartily, and that was Ina's first hearty laugh for months.

"And now," said Ina when the merriment had subsided, and Bert, who had in a great measure regained her composure, was seated on a chair opposite her, "please tell me why you called yourself my girl lover."

"Because I am," said Bert earnestly, now looking straight into the eyes she admired so much. "Don't you believe girls fall in love with each other? Miss Mulock shows in her dear, sad, delightful book, 'A Brave Lady,' that *she* thinks one woman may love another with the deepest and truest affection she is capable of feeling; and don't you know that Sophie May made Emily say that she was just as truly in love with Delight Sanborn as ever Romeo was with Juliet? And," she added demurely, "I am really in love with you, so of course I need no other proof that a girl really loves one of her own sex sometimes."

"I don't know what a *true* lover is like," said Ina, her face clouding, and a little bitterness creeping into her tone.

"I'll teach you," said Bert brightly. "I can't go prancing around the country doing battle for you as the knights of old did for their ladies; and I'm really afraid if you got into the river farther than was safe I could not tug you out, for, as Samantha said by Josiah, I'm not very 'hefty.' But I can be true, and kind, and constant, and I've often thought that when one does the little daily things that keep the hearts of those he loves warm, and their spirits cheerful, it is much nobler and better than doing them a big favor once in a while and considering that his whole duty towards them is done. And if you'll take me for your lover, and like me a little, I feel sure I can make things pleasanter for you than they would otherwise be. I'm not exactly a beauty, but they say homely folks are always good. Judge of the merits of yours truly."

"Well," said Ina with a look that was good to see, "I think a girl lover may be something nice, and I will give you a trial. And I do like you so far. But oh!" she exclaimed vehemently, "don't deceive me *ever!* It is a terrible thing to be disappointed in one we care for!"

"I never will, truly, truly!" was Bert's emphatic reply.

Later the two were speaking of a newly published book.

"I rather liked the story," declared Bert, "but I got thoroughly out of patience with Adele. It seemed so wrong and silly for her to be forever tormenting herself because she once loved Clarkson."

"But he was not worthy of her affection, and did not return it, you remember," said Ina.

"What of that?" answered Bert. "He *seemed* worthy, and it is no disgrace to love a good man who does not return the love, any more than it would be to love a good woman who did not return the affection. And even if it had been a disgrace, there was something better for her to do than sit moping and moaning. She raised the storm she seemed so powerless under, herself. It was with herself, and not with him, she had to do. It seems to me she ought to have stood right up against the gale, and made herself realize that she brought it on, and fought her way back to self-respect. She had no *right* to let herself go down lower, no right to stay where she was. God never meant it so. She was drowning in a sea of helplessness and folly, not because she had fallen into it, but because she allowed herself to stay there. But I must go now. It is near tea-time."

As she arose Ina arose too, and taking her guest's hand, she said pathetically, —

"I am afraid I have been foolish and helpless too, but have patience with me, little friend, lots of patience."

Bert hadn't an idea what her charmer's words meant, but she was bound to be loyal under any circumstances, and replied heartily, —

"Dear heart, you shall find me a real female Job for patience. Good-by, sweetheart, and you may trust me — always."

A sweet, serious look had come into the gray eyes. It was *Bertha* who spoke the last words, Bertha who held her friend's hand a moment at parting, and went away feeling that she had accepted a sacred trust.

"God never meant it so — in *her* case or mine," repeated Ina when she was alone. She was glad of these words that had come to her. "Of course not; why should he? Real Hilton reasoning that, little Bert. He never meant it, and has hindered it, and I *will* 'face the gale.'"

She went home, and praised the tea biscuits and helped, after supper, to clear the table. These were the "things of the moment."

CHAPTER X.

EVERY-DAY DOINGS.

"A commonplace life," we say, and we sigh;
But why should we sigh as we say?
The commonplace sun in the commonplace sky
Makes up the commonplace day.
And God, who studies each separate soul,
Out of commonplace lives makes his beautiful whole.

SUSAN COOLIDGE.

BERT HILTON was the petted niece of a rich man. Her every wish was gratified, and much money was given her. She dressed plainly, however, and the poor of the town knew where most of her funds went. In the bosoms of their families, or to particular friends, many who knew the ways of the Hiltons called both Rex and Bert "exceedingly eccentric," but took care to add that they were to be respected and honored for their generosity to the needy. Although the Hiltons never spoke in public of their charitable deeds, the grateful recipients of their bounty spread the name and fame of their benefactors abroad.

Bert, who could choose her associates from all Millerville, constituted herself the special friend of the telegraph operator at the station, thinking her, as she probably was, the handsomest girl she had ever seen, her voice, as it may well have been, the most musical one to which she had ever listened, rating her intellect, and perhaps justly, above that of any one with whom she had talked. The two girls were very different in temperament. Ina's nature was an intense one; everything was of moment to her. She knew no little things. She could love strongly and hate fiercely. Bert could love as strongly as her friend; but she often declared that she was the "poorest hand in Christendom to hate anybody," for just as she "got well at it" something always came up to make her forgive the offender, or at least pity him, or, worst of all, find him too weak to be worthy of anything but contempt, and so an end was put to the wrath she "meant should be so magnificent a thing."

Ina was feeling her way, looking with a faith that was half questioning at the Father, looking for signs that might prove her Lord's truth, but eager for the bread of life. Bert had simply put herself into God's hands, and did not care for sight since her faith was so strong. That the two should be friends was part of the "adjusting."

I wonder why it is that we can easily tell to comparative strangers what we find it so hard to disclose to those of our own blood or households; why the shy maiden whispers her love secret to a friend rather than to a sister; why the boy or young man discloses his cherished dream to a favorite "chum," but not to parents or brother.

In a month from the time when the two girls met, Bert Hilton knew more of Ina's real self, more of the inner workings of her mind, than the Winters had ever learned. One day Ina spoke of her summer dream and all its consequences.

Bert became Bertha as she listened. She wound her arm around her friend's waist, and when there had been silence for a few seconds, said gravely, —

"How surely are we in trouble from the very first 'shalt not' of God that we disobey, whether it is spoken through his word or by our consciences! How easy it is to *say* we 'shall not surely die,' and to go on dying all the while; dying to honor, to righteousness, to peace, to refinement, in order to retain something that is not worth keeping!

I will not say it was nothing, I *cannot*, dear, for I believe it was much. I believe the womanliness you bartered when you stole out to meet the man you had no right to meet was worth a thousand times more than his regard. The self-respect you laid aside was more than the pleasure you gained. *Nothing* is worth gaining that must be bought by making one's self less true, less noble, less upright. It *must* be so. How can those who are not pure in heart see God? And if they cannot see him how can they follow him? But you are quite free to-day, are you not, dear, from — *all* the unworthiness of that summer's so-called friendship? You are not building any hopes upon it? not keeping in your heart any plans or dreams of what might possibly still come of it, or *he* might become?"

Ina's head rose proudly, and her eyes shone as she answered, —

"Do you suppose I could call it repentance if I gave up something that it was wrong for me to hold, but still strove or hoped to keep it near my hand so that I could re-take it if I should change my mind. Do you think I would consider a gift worth trying to hold that was broken, defaced, and unworthy because *some time* it might become through some means better? that I would *hope* to marry a man whose past I must cover up, and be secretly ashamed of? Bert, hear me now, and believe me, and then we will never allude to this subject again. That summer and its unworthiness and weakness shall be as utterly as possible blotted out; as nearly as may be as though it had never been. I will go on with my life work, without reaching out for what *might* be, doing the clean, pure, honest thing of *now*, and please God I will win my dearest possessions back again."

The two girls took long walks and sometimes long rides together, and on Sundays Ina usually went to church and then home with Bert.

One evening they rode away from the village as soon as it was time for Ina to close her office. They entered a forest road along which they had for some distance rambled on foot, and drove on and on. The road became scarcely more than a path as they went on. Overhead the leaves were whispering to the branches, and looking down one saw springing from the turf the sweet little flowers that bloom in the shade.

"Isn't this glorious?" exclaimed Bert, driving

over a stump near the wheel track and nearly upsetting the buggy, thereby causing great clutching of the fender to keep from falling out.

"If you mean your driving, I'm sorry not to agree with you," said Ina, straightening her hat which had been thrown over her face.

"Well, we did have rather a hard scratch to keep in," said Bert, "but my thoughts were so elevated I couldn't bring them down to anything so earthy as that stump. But I'll be a model of prudence hereafter."

By and by they came into the open country, and rode on two miles farther, each heartily enjoying the clear air, the rapid motion, and all the spring beauty around them.

They took a circuitous route home, and when about a mile from the village, driving through a narrow road, they met a carriage. It was quite dark by this time, and in allowing the team to pass, Bert turned her horse too far to one side. The carriage drove rapidly away, and in trying to regain the road a wheel of Bert's buggy came in sharp contact with a rock by the wayside, and was instantly broken. Luckily the horse was not nervous, and the instant the accident occurred stood motionless. Bert clung to the side of the vehicle and Ina to the fender, the former exclaiming wildly, —

"'Angels and ministers of grace defend us!' This ill-mannered wheel has gone and splintered itself. Now I'm worse off than the man who went to London to buy him a wife, for I haven't even a wheelbarrow to get you home on."

"Never mind me," said Ina. "It can't be over three-quarters of a mile to the village, and we can easily walk that distance. But how shall we get the team home?"

"Oh, I'll lead Prince, and send Dennis after the carriage," said Bert easily, "but I'm dreadfully sorry you should have this tramp, for you must be tired."

They got the horse free from the carriage, and Bert led him. She led Ina too, saying she knew "every inch of the way;" but in a low place they walked directly into a deep mud puddle made by a shower the day before, and Prince's hoofs sent a quantity of mud over one of Ina's prettiest dresses.

"'This day all things begun come to ill end,'" declared Bert tragically when all had splashed out of the water, and Prince was waiting for the girls to stamp the mud off their boots.

In spite, or maybe partially because, of their mishaps, both girls declared they had had a delightful time, and in less than a week rode over the same ground again.

From Bert's love and care, and all that came of it, sprang health of body and mind for Ina. To the handsome, homelike house of the Hiltons she often went, a welcome guest, privileged to use its books, to carry away as many flowers as she liked from the gardens attached to it, to roam through its rooms, and dream away hours on its downy sofas or in its deep windows.

The older Hiltons were kind, true, helpful friends. She *felt* it. And Bert was her girl lover, her shadow, her companion; and the love of the strong, passionate girl went out to the tender little soul living her beautiful, merry life as though there was nothing else to be thought of but being true and good and noble in the girlish way set before her.

One day after several months of this intercourse with the Hiltons, Ina leaned her face on her hands and said a little earnest prayer, and then taking up her pen, began her story for girls.

CHAPTER XI.

MADGE'S ENGAGEMENT.

Cursed be the social wants that sin against the strength of youth!
Cursed be the social lies that warp us from the living truth!

TENNYSON.

SILVER BEACH was much gayer that season than it had ever been before. People were beginning to learn what a charming place it was; and those who loved quiet, and still wished to be near the sea, grumbled at the large crowds which gathered in the hotel parlors or on the piazzas, or promenaded on the beach.

One afternoon early in July two young men were sitting in one of the best-appointed rooms of the hotel they chose to patronize.

"Have you seen the new party?" inquired Tom Holt, carefully knocking the ashes from the end of his cigar.

"There are several new parties here," said Matthewson listlessly. "To which do you refer?"

"I mean the telegraph operator," answered

Tom. "If telegraph operators were in my line I should cultivate her acquaintance, for she's pretty as a pink, and her style just suits me."

"I have seen her," said Matthewson shortly, his listlessness all gone.

Holt looked at his friend in surprise. Matthewson was an amiable young man, and seldom spoke in the tone he had just used.

"Well, Sir Harry, I s'pose there's no harm in asking a question or expressing an opinion," he said.

"You have a perfect right to do either," said Matthewson stiffly, "but I do not care to discuss Miss Munroe."

And without another word he arose and left the room.

"Whew! How crusty we are, all at once!" exclaimed Holt, and after a moment added, —

"Miss Munroe. So that's the lady's name. I'll bet my last dollar against a five-cent piece that my high and mighty friend is interested to an uncommon degree in Miss M. Wish I had half his money, I'd see what I could do in the way of a flirtation with her just to pay him for his crustiness, if nothing more; but being as poor as a church mouse I must spend my time looking for some one who can come down with the stamps to pay my bills and give me something to jingle in my pockets."

And after pocketing half a dozen of Matthewson's Havanas, he too arose, and sauntered out.

Matthewson went out of the house and down to the beach with a feeling of anger towards Holt in his heart that he knew was strange and unreasonable. Tom had spoken of Miss Munroe as he himself had often spoken of other young ladies; but somehow the careless words jarred on him, and he resented them. He did not want Madge Munroe to be talked over by such men as Holt.

He had seen Madge a number of times; once or twice in the hall, several times in the dining-room, and twice he had sent telegrams and exchanged business words with her. This was all their intercourse, but he knew that he had never met a woman who awoke within him such feelings as did this girl.

"I feel she is womanly and true," he said, looking out over the sea.

And then there came to him a vague wish that he was more manly and true. He had done nothing the world condemned, but what good thing had he done? What had he to offer a woman that would be an adequate return for a pure, white heart?

Strange thoughts these for Matthewson, whose moral character had never troubled him before.

"Can it be that I am in love with this girl?" he asked himself. But he was not prepared to answer the question; and the sky above, and the rocks and sea below, which were his only companions, gave no reply.

There was a great deal of work to be done in the Silver Beach telegraph office that summer. The telegraph served many heads of firms who could not neglect their business even while taking much-needed rest. Numerous messages of a social nature were sent and received. Madge found time to think of little but business. She was glad to have this so. She did not want to think of the past, and her dreams of the future did not now take as fair shapes as they were wont to do a year before. One day, when she had been at Silver Beach little more than a week, she sat, during a momentary lull of business, before her desk, thinking intently, when there was a sharp rap on the little shelf behind her on which blanks and pen and ink for customers were kept. She arose and pushed the message window open, expecting to see a customer, but no person was in sight. There was a sound of hurrying feet in the hall, and before her lay the most exquisite bouquet she had ever seen. She took it up with an exclamation of surprise, and then the thought came to her that probably there was some mistake, that the flowers were not for her. But nestling among the lovely blossoms was a tiny slip of paper; and thinking it might explain to whom the bouquet belonged, and that she would send it by the message boy, she took the note in her hand and opened it. The words she read were: —

"Will Miss Munroe accept these blossoms from one who wishes to be her friend?"

The brief missive was signed H. M.

Madge was passionately fond of flowers, and the same look of delight and admiration shone in her eyes as had come to them on that morning, which seemed so long ago, when she found the rose beside her plate.

She could but accept this gift or leave the

flowers to wither on the slab. She could not bear to do the latter, and then she asked herself why should she not accept them? So she placed their stems in water, and until they withered they gave her a sense of companionship that was grateful to her.

A day or two after this occurrence Henry Matthewson had occasion to send a message. As Madge took the telegram from his hand her cheeks flushed, for she recognized the handwriting she saw; it was the same as that on the slip of paper that was found among the flowers. Timidly she mentioned the gift, and asked if she might not thank him for it. Matthewson acknowledged himself the donor, and begged that she would not think him presumptuous.

"It seemed to me you must need something to cheer you while you worked so steadily in this little den," he said.

The words and thought were kind, and Madge was pleased with them. She thanked him, and the two stood for some minutes talking together. As Madge was arranging the blanks on the shelf before her, her hand for an instant touched Matthewson's, which was toying with a pencil. He felt a thrill go through him, and the blood rush to his very forehead, and considered that the question asked on the beach was answered.

Thus began his acquaintance with Madge. It may seem strange that he had never met her in Brentwood, but such was the case. Her business had confined her closely to her office, and he had spent but little time in the village. Hunting, fishing, and, more than all, his "friend of a summer" had absorbed his attention so completely that it is not to be wondered at that those two met for the first time at Silver Beach. It was not long after that meeting that the gossips began to whisper that young Matthewson "really seemed much interested in that telegraph operator. Wouldn't it be queer if — but of course it was only a flirtation. He couldn't mean anything. His mother and sisters were proud as Lucifer, and nobody seemed to know anything about her family," etc.

But Matthewson *did* mean something by his attention. He had pretended to be in love with many, now he was honestly in love with one. He had but little thought for anybody but Madge, and sought her company at every available opportunity. He felt that unless he could win her for his wife life would hold for him little joy and no satisfying pleasure. He knew his mother and sisters were proud, very proud, and would probably object to his marrying a girl who for years had earned a livelihood for herself, but not for a moment did he abandon or waver in his determination to do so if she could be won by him.

His flowers constantly filled two beautiful vases he had one day given her. Delicious fruits bought by him found their way to her desk; the newest books and latest magazines — which she seldom found time to look into — were kept within reach of her hand.

As for her it may be said she drifted with the current which the tide of circumstances made.

"I will let things take their course," she said wearily. "I am tired of thinking and planning, and, after all, we cannot change Fate's decrees, struggle as we may."

She did not reason, as she had been so apt to do in the old days, that we make, in a great measure, our own fate; shape our own lives with our own wills and hands.

It was one evening after she had closed the office and had been walking on the beach with

Matthewson, and had stopped to rest at a place quite away from the other promenaders, and near one of those "blue inlets" of which Read sings, that she received her second offer of marriage.

Her lover's words were many and well chosen. His passion made him eloquent. But her heart did not quicken its beating or her cheeks take a deeper color as she listened. There was no glad, sweet joy at knowing this man loved her. She was truthful by nature. She made no pretence of being surprised at the declaration to which she had just listened; but when Matthewson bent over her and asked, "Is it to be yes, Madge?" she looked in his face and said, —

"Mr. Matthewson, you have been most kind to me, and I am grateful to you, and I like you for a friend, but I do not love you at all."

"But you will, you *must* in time, if you will only allow me to teach you to do so!" he cried. "Why, darling, it seems to me that such love as mine will surely *compel* a return. Shall it be as I wish, dear?"

Again to Madge came the vision of that early home, and the tired mother who had not lived out more than half her days, and in contrast the dream-home which she and Josie had builded, and which this man's money could make a reality. There could be no mistake about his wealth. She had heard it spoken of too many times to believe it a myth. And then she had noticed that the deference which is paid to riches was accorded him.

"It may be as he says, that I shall learn to love him, to love him, and to forget" — And then, as if fearful if she faltered she might refuse him, she held out her hand without a word. It was seized by Matthewson, held for a second to his lips, and when he released it a beautiful diamond gleamed on its third finger.

CHAPTER XII.

TELLING MOTHER.

Be ruled by me, forget to think of her.

SHAKESPEARE.

"AND so it is all settled. Well, Henry, I am really glad. Is it Miss Fairbanks, or Lillie Sprague? I suppose it is one or the other. They say there's no end to Fairbanks's money, but I do think the Spragues are more cultured if somewhat less wealthy. Both good families, my dear. Which is it, Henry?"

Mrs. Matthewson's face was full of approval as she beamed serenely on the one son of her family, who lay stretched at full length on the sofa. The son raised himself slowly to a sitting posture, and looking down and speaking hesitatingly, as though abashed at uttering such new thoughts, he said, —

"Might there not be other things besides wealth and family to recommend a woman? Might not one marry a woman for her purity and worth, and forget whether she was wealthy or not? marry her for his great love's sake, and not care to know whom she called father or grandfather ?"

At his words Mrs. Matthewson's look of approval changed to one of astonishment, and she said quickly, —

"What do you mean by your sentimental questions ? Are you not engaged to one of the girls I have mentioned ?

"Thank heaven, *no !*" cried Matthewson.

"Then to whom *are* you engaged ?" cried Mrs. Matthewson. "I *do* hope you have not done anything foolish."

"Mother," said Matthewson, "I have money enough in my own right to make a wife comfortable. You know I have spent but little of what uncle Charles left me. I don't covet any woman's fortune, but I do covert one woman, a fair, beautiful woman, whose dearest possession is her white heart ; the daughter of a farmer in the State of New York ; an orphan now, and at present telegraph operator at Silver Beach. Her name is Madge Munroe."

It would be impossible to describe the look with which Mrs. Matthewson received this reply. Dismay, anger, and astonishment were in it. For a moment she was silent, and then she said in a hard, constrained tone,—

"What *shall* I say to this exhibition of low taste and utter foolishness? A pretty daughter to think of bringing *me!* I suppose she has no more idea of what makes a lady than my Nora has, and perhaps not as much, for Nora has been in my family for some time and has had an opportunity to learn many things from your sisters and me. I can imagine this girl with her cheap clothing and jewelry. Men can't tell what women wear, but I'll warrant you she would disgrace us all with her tawdriness and vulgarity."

"Stop!" cried Matthewson sternly; "I will not hear Madge Munroe spoken of as you are speaking of her. I should be proud of my sisters were they like her in appearance and manner. I do not know or care what any of her garments cost. I only know she is always well and tastefully dressed. She wears no jewelry but her pretty gold watch and my ring. And I tell you now I had rather she wore that ring than any other woman on the face of the globe."

Mrs. Matthewson, finding that scornful words would not effect her purpose, chose to assume a very affectionate manner and tone. Going to the sofa she sat down beside her son, and passing her hand fondly over his arm, she said, —

"My dear boy, this young person may be well enough, but if you reflect a moment you will see how foolish a thing marrying her would be. What would people say if you, who could choose a wife from the wealthiest and most aristocratic young ladies of the city, should make a life companion of a poor working-girl?"

"I *have* reflected a good deal," said Matthewson, "and I can see no reason why the girl I love should not be my wife. I don't care what people say."

"But, Henry," said Mrs. Matthewson, "if you do not care to keep from so foolish a thing as a marriage with this girl would be for your own sake, think of the feelings of your family, who of course would be obliged to receive her as daughter and sister. Do break your mad engagement."

"I will spare you all the mortification of receiving her," replied Matthewson. "I will take her to some place where we both shall be likely to be happier than we could be near here. I can do as I please with the money uncle Charles left me, so there will be no 'love in a cottage' affair for us."

Mrs. Matthewson talked until she was convinced that words were thrown away on her obstinate son, and then left the room, and seeking her two daughters, who had just returned from a shopping expedition, told them the dreadful news that their brother had become engaged to a poor girl, the daughter of a farmer, and at present working in a telegraph office.

"And does he imagine you will ever call this low-born creature daughter, or we sister?" exclaimed Helen loftily.

"Why, it's downright abominable!" exclaimed Hortense.

"I dare say," said Mrs. Matthewson, "that she has led Henry on by those arts which that class of people know so well how to employ until he really fancies himself in love with her. He may see his folly before it is too late. I cannot yet believe that a descendant of the Lesters will stoop so low as to marry a telegraph operator. I'll warrant you your father won't say a word against this engagement. Henry takes his romantic notions and low tastes from the Matthewsons."

As his wife had predicted, Mr. Matthewson, senior, did not "say a word" against his son's intended marriage. His mind went back to his own young manhood, and recalled the image of a fair girl whose face used to brighten at his approach and sadden when he went away. He remembered the happy hours he had spent planning for his own future and that of her who loved him. The pride of his family came between him and his humble idol, and he married a woman cold, haughty, and wealthy, and the world called him fortunate. No, he had not a word to say against his son's choice. And yet among them all, the scheming mother, the arrogant daughters, the father who had married for wealth, there was not one to whom came the thought that this girl who had labored honorably all her life, and thus earned an honorable place in the world, whose soul was clear from blame, whose purposes, if mistaken, were still earnest and unselfish, would, by giving herself to this elegant loafer, who had always pleased himself without regard to others, to whom good impulses came like flitting shadows, only to be quickly blown aside, was bartering her birthright for a mess of pottage; that she was giving much for no legitimate return; that she was not demanding what it was her right and duty to expect from one who asked her hand.

CHAPTER XIII.

WEARY DAYS.—SILVER BEACH.

Our souls are filled with earthly dust,
  The glory fades from our skies away,
And the human heart, like the mountain pine,
  Sings a song of grief on the brightest day.

AUGUSTUS M. LORD.

A NEIGHBOR, come on some trifling errand, stood one morning on John Winter's back door-step, and told Mrs. Winter a bit of news which she had forgotten while in the house, and Mark, standing at the kitchen sink washing his hands, heard her words. Mrs. Winter went directly up-stairs to make the beds after the neighbor's departure. She hoped her son had not heard Mrs. Green's last bit of information. It might be an idle story, and perhaps Mark would mind it. Anyway, there was no use troubling him yet, whether it was true or false. Thus thought the mother as she shook up pillows and smoothed sheets and counterpanes.

A handsome and wealthy young man, whose

name the neighbor had not heard, paying marked attention to Madge Munroe!

Sky, you may be soft, and blue, and tender, or veil yourself in threatening clouds. You are unnoted.

The young man seems much in love, and she evidently favors his suit.

Beautiful flush of sunrise, gorgeous glow of sunset, you are unnoticed and count for naught.

Everybody thought the marriage of the two would take place.

Green living things, sparkling brooks, and singing birds, how are you neglected! Your once lover is unseeing, unhearing.

"It is all right, and I will bear it like a man, please God!"

As the long, slow, summer days went by Mark said these words many times; said them when he could speak them, sobbed them when his voice would not be controlled. Day after day, week after week, he suffered on, unable to put his great love aside, unable to make the madness that came with it less, not because he was weak, but because he was terribly strong. It was not weakness but strength, the strength of his whole character, the intensity of his soul, the earnestness of all his nature, that made him sometimes throw his scythe or rake aside and hide himself in some secluded spot, and weep as only the strong can weep; that again and again drove him to his knees to cry out for pardon for not being ready to give up what evidently was not for him; that wrung from his lips many times each day the prayer, —

"Lord, dear Lord, I am *not* willing, but oh! I am ready, anxious to be *made* willing!"

Had he been a weak man he could have philosophized of the matter. He could have told himself it was a pity, and that really he had loved her very dearly and truly. But as long as she chose to be wooed by another it was of no use to be fretting about her, no use to make himself miserable. He might have repeated for his consolation that proverb, — manufactured, it seems to me, for the express use of vapid-minded people, — "There are as good fish in the sea as ever were caught." Madge Munroe was not *a* woman to him, and the thought did not once occur to him that as long as she could or would not be his some one else could and would. There were other women doubtless as pure and true, undoubtedly as fair, but nevertheless Madge Munroe was, would always be, *the* woman of all the world to Mark Winter. He would never be reconciled in a way that would take from him one whit of his manliness. "I will bear it like a man, please God!" These were his words. And he *did* bear it like a man, like a strong, loving, tortured, suffering man. He did not complain, and no one heard his sobbings or outcries. Sometimes his hands would drop their work for sheer lack of power to go on with the task in hand; but the power was resolutely called back, and he labored on because it was a duty rather than that toil was agreeable. His hands worked with no stimulation from his heart.

He realized now there had always been in his heart a thought and hope which he had never put into words even to himself, that Madge might yet some time care for him, might come to him as his wife. It was the killing of this thought, this hope, that smote him so sorely.

One day, when he had suffered for weeks, and was on his knees urging the old request, pleading to be made willing to give up what was dearer to him than life, new thoughts came to him. What if God did not want him to be willing? What if his prayers were not answered in the way he had hoped or expected — Mark believed in some kind of answer to prayer — because he was not willing to settle down and let things take their course? What if Madge was in danger? Handsome and rich men were not necessarily good and true men. What if she was to be saved from the impending marriage, and — oh! happy thought!— that *he* was to save her? He tried to put the thoughts by, but they remained and repeated themselves again and again.

"Do not mock me, Lord!" he cried with his face turned skyward. And over and over the thoughts were repeated in his mind.

It was about four o'clock when he left the field, and going to the house sought his mother, and told her he was going to Silver Beach on the morrow.

"Do you think it best, my son?" asked Mrs. Winter anxiously.

"Yes, I think it was shown to me that it was —out there by the brook. Aren't you willing, mother?"

Mrs. Winter put her hand on Mark's arm, and asked, —

"Did you hear what Mrs. Green said when she called here a few weeks ago? Have you heard, my boy, that Madge is probably engaged?"

She had noticed Mark's growing pallor and abstraction, but had hoped it might be the heat that affected him. She had shrunk from questioning him. She did not know that Madge had refused him. Perhaps he did not hear the story of Mrs. Green, and was going to Silver Beach to ask Madge to marry him. Would it not be better for him to hear of this probable engagement at home than to learn it at that crowded place? She had thought things out before she spoke. And Mark answered her, —

"Yes, I heard what Mrs. Green said. I don't know *why* I am to go to Silver Beach. Perhaps it is an illusion, but I feel that I am to go; that I was *ordered* there."

On the morrow he started. He did not know what to do with himself when he arrived at that glittering watering-place. The man of wide fields and solitary places was lost and amazed in that small spot with its crowds of people. He had no plans. He did not know how to find out if the handsome rich man was good and true. He had not seen him, did not know his name. But he was here to learn what he did not know. He must wait. He did not seek Madge. He did not deem it best. He went down to the beach, and sat watching the waves and the children at play on the rocks and sand till it was nearly dark. It was half-past eight when, after partaking of a light hotel supper, he stepped out upon the long piazza and into the shade which some thick vines growing near the end of it made. He had stood there but a few minutes when Madge Munroe, leaning on the arm of a gentleman, came out and began promenading up and down the piazza. The electric light made the place like noonday, and her face could be distinctly seen. For a moment Mark looked only at Madge, looked at her eagerly, wistfully, as though he would fill his soul full of her image. She put her hand to her head to brush back a lock of hair loosened by the breeze, and he noticed the costly ring that sparkled on her finger. And then he looked at her companion, and started quickly, looked at him again sharply and steadily, and drew a long inward breath, and muttered to himself: "It is that Matthewson — again! Everything for him! It wasn't enough that he should almost break our Ina's heart, and kill her outright. He must palm himself off as an honest man on Madge, and get for himself the love that would make heaven for me, and that I'd die for if there was any need of it. O Lord, it *does* seem strange and hard! I don't understand."

The promenaders came near him more than once in their walk. He noticed how carefully Matthewson kept the wrap about Madge's shoulders, how lovingly he looked into her eyes, and whispered between his closed teeth: "The hypocrite! the black-souled villain! Why hasn't somebody told her? Some of these people must know him. Hasn't there been a single one kind enough to let her know the truth?"

O simple Mark! what would you have said could you have heard it whispered, as it often was, that Madge was an "exceedingly lucky girl to insnare young Matthewson"? How it would have amazed and puzzled you had you heard it said, as it frequently was, that Matthewson had had "several little affairs of the heart, but then young men would *be* young men, and youthful sins must be winked at!" You would have asked probably, and been laughed at for your pains, *why* young men who should be full of good impulses and high, clean hopes, who are not embittered by trials or hardened by excessive toil, must be pardoned for being sinful. Evidently, Mark, you were not of the world; at least, the fashionable world.

No, the handsome, rich man was not good and true, not fit to be *her* husband. But what could be done? How could he of all people go to her and tell her of her lover's character? The very love that prompted the doing of this stood between the wish and the act. In what light would she regard statements coming from a would-be lover against an actual lover? He must wait. His way was not clear.

He was a little disappointed in Madge, though he tried hard to excuse her. How was it that her fineness did not rise up instinctively to repel what perhaps was not coarseness, but what it seemed to him must show as *un*fineness in Matthewson? How could it be that his lack of genuine manhood did not show itself? Could water always *seem* clear when its fountain was corrupt? Could Madge tolerate anything that was not genuine? Could wealth tempt her to marry a man she did not wholly respect, truly love?

He felt himself unloyal as these questions asked themselves, and tried to defend Madge in his thoughts against his thoughts.

He went into the house leaving the two sitting on the piazza. He sought his room, clear only on one point: the man to whom Madge was engaged was *not* a good, true man.

CHAPTER XIV.

MARK'S OPPORTUNITY.—A PROMISE.

Dream not helm and harness
  The sign of valor true;
Peace hath higher tests of manhood
  Than battle ever knew.

WHITTIER.

Gratitude is expensive.

GIBBON.

THE day was an exceedingly hot one even at Silver Beach where the sea-breeze was doing its best to make a comfortable atmosphere. White cloud-heads were rearing themselves in the west, and some of the few who were abroad remarked that there would be thunder before night. But as yet the afternoon sun was unclouded, fierce, and pitiless. The ladies, for the most part, were asleep in their rooms. The gentlemen lounged in large numbers on the piazzas, smoking, reading, talking about the weather, doing all in a half-hearted way for which the heat was responsible.

In a cove something more than a quarter of a mile below the main landing at Silver Beach, a small wharf had been constructed by a fisherman who lived a mile away from the shore. He had sometimes found it almost impossible to land upon the open beach on account of the surf, and so had made this tiny wharf in a place where the water was comparatively still. On the day of which I speak a small boat was fastened to one of the piers of the fisherman's wharf, and lying in it, with his arm under his head, and his face covered by his panama hat, was Henry Matthewson, fast asleep. Listless and uncomfortable, he had wandered down to the beach in search of coolness, wishing it was evening and Madge free to come out with him; thinking that another summer would not find her pent up in an office, but in the Old World visiting places she longed to see and he wished to show her. He wandered on until he found the cove and saw the boat tied to the wooden pier. It might be cooler in the boat, he thought; and very soon he had pulled it toward him, stepped into it, and was stretched at full length. It *was* cooler there, and he liked the sound of the water against the side of the boat.

Still dreaming of and planning for that trip to the Old World with Madge as his wife, he fell asleep.

And when he had slept a half-hour some one came near to the cove, and, without seeing the wharf or boat, sat down on a rock and looked out over the sea. It was Mark Winter, who had been two days at Silver Beach. On this third day he was very restless and unhappy. He had not approached Madge, had not let her know he was there. He felt that it would surely lower him as well as Matthewson in her eyes were he to go to her and tell her of her lover's summer friend; for would it not be regarded as something told as much to destroy Matthewson's chance of winning her, that he might have a better hope of winning her himself, as to defend her against an unworthy suitor? He probed his own heart to its depths, and sifted his own hopes and intentions like wheat; and looking out over the water he said earnestly, as though the waves had accused him,—

"I don't expect her to marry *me*. She must love wealth and gayety, or I believe she could not have accepted him. I have thought much about that since I came here. I must not think she would marry an old plodder like me. She can do better, and I will not blame her, and I wouldn't, so help me Heaven! *think* of putting a thing in the way if he was a good man; and I won't, no, *never*, thrust myself upon her notice if I can help it. But I mustn't stand by and see her marry an unworthy man and not try to stop it. But how am I going to let her know what is true? Would she *believe* the story I would tell her coming from *me?* And must I lose her respect as well as do without her love? O Lord, Lord, show me the way!"

And then he began to tell himself that if no other way was revealed to him, it would clearly be his *duty* to make known to Madge Matthewson's treachery; to show to her as clearly as might be what manner of man she had promised to wed; to put himself in a position where he might be misunderstood, and consequently despised. He must think of her, not of himself. He must do his duty, but would the Father show him no way but this? Oh that Madge would justify his old-time faith in her by feeling the unmanliness of Matthewson, and seeking to know from whence the feeling sprung; that the fine instinct with which he had credited her might rise as a barrier, which could not be torn down, between her womanliness and his base nature; that she might not be obliged to see her lover through another's eyes to know his unworthiness!

Not one whit of his faith in Madge would Mark let go without a struggle. He would far rather have loved and never gained for his own a noble woman, than to feel that his love for the woman he once would have married must die because there was not enough of the element of respect in it to keep it alive.

While he was thinking these things the white clouds had become dark and risen until their edges touched the zenith. A sharp gust of wind swept over the water, and the little boat rocked rapidly from side to side, but still Matthewson slept; and Mark, quite unconscious that one near him was in peril, looked up at the heavens and decided that he must start for the hotel at once if he would reach it before the storm came on. But he was scarcely on his feet before, with a dash of rain, came another and a fiercer blast. There was a sound of strands giving way, a final strain, and the rope that had held the boat was severed, and the tiny craft swept far out into the sea which was boiling and bubbling with the fury of the sudden gale. Matthewson, now fully awake, uttered a loud and dismayed exclamation, and Mark's eyes were instantly turned upon him. There was no keeping one's place in that tossing boat amidst those tumultuous waves, and Matthewson was soon struggling in the water. He was but an indifferent swimmer, and, after a few spasmodic efforts in his own behalf, went down. By this time Mark had thrown off his coat and waistcoat, and was making his way as fast as possible to where he had seen Matthewson. Mark was an excellent swimmer, but the odds against him were terrible. When Matthewson came up, however, he was near him, and soon was clutching his clothing with one hand and striking out for the shore with the disengaged arm. It was hard, dreadfully hard, pulling against that surging sea with one arm and so heavy a burden, for Matthewson was but semiconscious, and could do nothing for himself; but the strength of ten seemed to be within Mark. He struggled and fought against the tide, ever getting a little nearer the shore. There was help for him presently. The man who owned the wharf and boat, fearing the latter might be swept out to sea, had come down to the shore to secure it. He took in the situation, and plunging into the sea, which was growing calmer, he swam out to meet the two men.

"Take *him!*" said Mark, who was nearly exhausted; and the fisherman grasped the unconscious man and soon had him on the beach. A moment more, and Mark too was on the beach; and he too was unconscious, and more, the blood was trickling from a small wound near his temple. Some floating object had struck him sharply on the head when he was near the shore. The fisherman left the two lying on the damp sand, and ran for help, and very soon those things which are always done for half-drowned people were being done for Matthewson, and Mark was taken rapidly to the Clarendon House, where some one said he boarded, and a physician summoned.

There was no listlessness about Silver Beach now. People crowded about the Clarendon House exclaiming and explaining, asking questions, giving answers, right or wrong ones, and waiting for the doctor's verdict. Madge Munroe in her office learned the cause of the tumult, and heard some one say the name of the man who saved Matthewson was Webster.

The physician declared that Matthewson would be all right in a few hours, but that Mr. Winter — the doctor had learned from the hotel clerk that the brave gentleman's name was Winter — was severely hurt and brain fever might be the result of his injuries.

Mark's consciousness came back about eight o'clock in the evening, and he lay tossing, raving, writhing, with his hands at his head, until the doctor administered a soothing draught which soon threw him into an uneasy sleep. Early in the morning Matthewson, who had begged hard for the privilege, was admitted to the sick man's room. Mark was awake and quite conscious. Matthewson stole quietly to the bed, for it was only on condition that he should not speak or make a noise that he was admitted. Mark saw and recognized him, and for several moments fixed his eyes upon him, and then beckoned the doctor to the side of the bed, and said, —

"Will you leave me alone with him a few minutes? I have something I must say to him alone."

"I don't want you to talk," said the physician.

"I *must* talk for ten minutes. After that I will be as quiet as you wish."

The doctor, seeing that to argue the point might do more harm than to yield it, turned away after assuring his patient that he should return to the room in ten minutes by his watch. As soon as he was gone, Mark turned to Matthewson and said,—

"What are you willing to do for me in return for what I did for you yesterday?"

"Anything," cried Matthewson impulsively. "If money can reward you"—

But Mark silenced him by a look, and said,—

"Listen. Only one thing will satisfy me, and I want you to promise me that *now;* for I heard the doctor say that I should probably have brain fever, and if I did, the chances were I should never survive it."

The haggard face was alive with earnestness, and the large eyes looked straight into his companion's.

"Do you promise *all* that I ask?"

"I solemnly promise," said Matthewson, never dreaming what that promise would cost.

"Go to Madge Munroe," said Mark, still looking intently into his companion's eyes, and speaking with all the strength he was master of, "and tell her all your past. Tell her, above all, of the child, Ina Ellerton, whom you wooed with no thought of wedding. Tell her the whole story just as it is. Tell her, too, of any others you have wooed in the same way. Tell her of all your habits. Let her know exactly the kind of man she is engaged to marry. I don't ask you to break your engagement, though you are not worthy of her; but I demand that she shall have a chance to judge of your character, and I ask that you give her this chance on the first opportunity."

Matthewson grew pale as Mark went on. He had met Mark but once in Brentwood, and had not recognized the sturdy farmer in his preserver, and when he had learned that Winter was the sick man's name, still failed to connect the name with Ina Ellerton's uncle of whom she used to speak so often. But now the truth flashed into his mind. This man, who demanded so terrible a promise from him, was Mark Winter, the uncle of his friend of a summer, and he, who prided himself on always keeping his word, had promised him something that might cost him his life happiness. What if he broke his word? Mark Winter *might* not die, or if he was near dying he might take measures to learn whether the promise had been kept, and if not, reveal himself to Madge what he wished her to know. Better, far better, that the lover should reveal his own secrets than that they should be revealed by another. And this man had saved his life, and asked this as his reward.

"Is there nothing else you can ask of me?" he cried. "Madge is a simple country girl. I cannot make her understand."

"Nothing else," said Mark. "Madge will understand with a right understanding. Remember you promised."

"Name any sum you will, and withdraw this promise," entreated Matthewson: "I will pay it to you or"—

Footsteps were coming towards the room. The ten minutes were up.

"A million dollars would not tempt me. I hold you to your promise," interrupted Mark.

The doctor's hand was on the door-knob. Matthewson, pale as the face on the pillow, looked into the steady, determined, gleaming eyes of the sick man, and cried,—

"I will keep my word, but Heaven help me!"

John and Sarah Winter were telegraphed for that morning. Madge Munroe, reading the telegram she was to transmit, learned who it was that had saved her lover. The man who brought the message thought she must be ill she looked so deathly white, and seemed so weak as she stood with the paper in her hand.

CHAPTER XV.

THE BRINK OF THE GRAVE. — THE PRAYER OF FAITH.

My shadow falls upon my grave,
So near the brink I stand.

HOOD.

Patience. . . . Have faith, and thy prayer will be answered.

LONGFELLOW.

"IS there any hope for my boy, doctor?"

The physician saw that no evasive reply would be accepted, and answered, looking at the hat in his hand rather than at his questioner, —

"There is really no hope for him, Mrs. Winter. I think there must have been something before that stroke on his head and this illness to sap his vitality. Somehow I cannot seem to stimulate him. His mind doesn't seem right, and you know how much the mind has to do with the health of the body. You had better send for his father. It will soon be over now."

Mark Winter had been sick ten days when this conversation took place. The gay watering-place life went on much as usual down-stairs, but the Clarendon House considerately had its hops in another building that the sick man might not be disturbed by the music. People came and went. The flirting and matchmaking continued. People slept in the morning and early afternoon, and danced till the small hours. And the ocean thundered on the beach, and caressed the pebbles with its waves.

Day after day had the sick one burned and raved and suffered, talking almost incessantly, revealing to his pitiful, tender nurse what a hard thing life had been to him since he had forgotten to notice the sky and the sunsets, and ceased to be the friend of the birds and flowers. He talked much of the ring he had seen glitter and shine on Madge's hand, and told the waves half-angrily that they did not understand; that he would *never* thrust himself upon her. He cried out to God to show him some other way than *this* way, and then groaned that if it was his duty he must not shirk it.

Day after day a patient woman had worked and prayed, and hoped against hope, asking patiently a patient God if it *could* not be his will to spare this *one* who was all that was left of all he had given her.

Day after day a girl had sat in her office regretting, hoping because she *would* hope, sending up to heaven youth's demanding prayer, "Father save him, for he *must not* die!"

As Mrs. Winter was on her way to the sick-room after hearing the doctor's verdict and asking him to send a telegram to her husband, she met a lady with whom she had once or twice exchanged a greeting, and who wore the soft, sober garb of the Friends. The lady stopped her and laid her hand on her shoulder.

"Thou art in trouble, friend," she said. "Is thy son worse?"

"The doctor says it cannot last long now," faltered Mrs. Winter.

"No doubt he has done his best," said the lady, "but hast *thou* tried the prayer of faith?"

The prayer of faith! *Had* she tried it? She had prayed to be sure; prayed so often and so earnestly; prayed with a great fear in her heart; prayed that the thing might not happen to which she begged to be resigned if it *must* happen. She thought of these things, and answered her questioner, —

"No, I don't think I *have* tried the prayer of *faith*."

"Wilt thou come into my room and pray with me?" said the lady. "I would have thee remember that the dear Lord has promised he will answer the united prayer of two or three."

The room was entered, the door closed, and on their knees the two gray-haired women prayed, one with ready, devout, believing, trustful words, while the other, down whose cheeks the tears were falling, could only cry brokenly, —

"For my son's life, O Lord! His dear life! Lord, I do believe. Help thou mine unbelief."

"Your son cannot live more than twenty-four hours." That was what Dr. Vander hâd telegraphed to John Winter.

At one o'clock Madge usually went into the dining-room, but this day she stole up to Mark Winter's room instead. Ina Ellerton, who had arrived a few hours before, sat by her uncle's bed. The two girls sadly greeted each other, and after a little Ina said, —

"Will you please sit by uncle Mark a few minutes while I go and see about my trunk? There is some trouble about it. I have persuaded grandma to lie down for a while."

Ina slipped away, and Madge took the chair she had vacated. Mark was quiet, and was in a stupor or a sleep. All the hectic of the fever had left his face, and it was deathly pale. The dark hair was thrown back from the forehead which showed so pitifully plain the blue veins. A groan occasionally escaped the pallid lips. Dr. Vander had told her that probably there would be no more realization of anything for his patient, and as she sat and looked at the fearfully changed face the terrible thought came to her that he would never look at her or speak to her again; and she longed with a passionate longing for one more look from eyes that had been so tender for her, one more word from lips that had ever spoken her name so kindly. Just one more look, one more word! Oh that it had come to this! that she must think that *only* one might be vouchsafed; that this one might be denied.

She arose and bent over Mark, fast asleep, or held fast by a stupor. Could she by any means arouse him?

"Mark," she whispered passionately, "Mark, will you not awaken? O my friend! can you not hear me? Can you not look at me? O Mark, my beloved! there is nothing stands between us now, and it is Madge who speaks; Madge whom you used to love. I was wrong, dear Mark; wrong and mistaken. I pained and hurt you, and you will go down into the grave and never know how sorry I am; never hear me say I love you. One more look, Mark, one more word for your own Madge!"

Where were you, Mark, when these words were spoken? Where was that soul of yours? You had not known of other things that had been said to you; why did you understand those passionate words? From what depths did they call you back? By what process were you made to hear and understand?

For he *did* hear and understand. Was it all a dream, or a fancy of his brain? He had had so many fancies of late! He opened his eyes. Ina opened the door as he did so, and hastened to his side. Madge was sitting beside him. And it was not death but life he wanted. Why should he die? "Mark, my beloved, there is nothing stands between us now."

Skies and sunsets, you may have your admirer again. He has heard the words of life, and he understands.

"I was wrong, dear Mark; wrong and mistaken. You will go down into your grave and never know how sorry I am; never hear me say I love you."

Birds and flowers, there is hope for you. Your friend may think of you lovingly again. Love's miracle has been performed. He will live.

"Is that you, Madge?" said Mark feebly. "And Ina too? I would like some water."

Madge had her look and word; commonplace enough, but oh! so precious! And at this look and word there sprung to her mind the glad thought that after all it might not be the last. Doctors were so often mistaken. Why should not Dr. Vander be? She would not believe it was the last. Please God he would look into her face and speak to her again.

At three o'clock Mrs. Winter awoke from a two hours' sleep, and rising quickly went to her son's room. She found Dr. Vander there standing beside his bed with a half-puzzled, wholly pleased look on his face.

"Mr. Winter seems to have taken a favorable turn," he said. "There is a better tone through all his system. I think he can rest now. I will call again in an hour."

"The prayer of faith shall heal the sick, and the Lord shall raise him up," said Mrs. Winter to herself. "How good God is!"

Do you say she was mistaken? that it was Madge's words that brought new life? You are right. It was Madge Munroe's words, but who shall say there was no connection between the prayer and the words? Who shall declare to us that it just *happened* that Madge Munroe bent over the dying and said those words? Does not God answer prayer by natural means? And is it less an answer because the means *are* natural?

It was one evening when it had begun to be whispered that Mark would undoubtedly die that Madge stood on the shore in the moonlight and heard the story of Matthewson's summer friendship. He told the story as it was. Somehow when he would have held something back and prevaricated, that pale, stern face came before him obliging him to tell the whole truth. There were other things to tell, but this one friendship was what Madge seemed most deeply interested in.

When the tale was finished she stood silent, and he went on explaining, protesting, telling her such things happened every season in society;

that it was considered nothing by most people. He asked her to overlook what seemed so wrong to her now but would seem trivial when she knew more of the world. He protested that he meant to be different, *so* different hereafter; that she had made a new man of him.

And at last Madge answered him, —

"It was a hard, cruel, wrong thing to do; but I can more easily forgive you because I have been hard and cruel and wrong myself. It has all come to me clearly and strongly as I stood here: you did not love this girl, but you taught her to love you. I did not love you, but I allowed you to put the betrothal ring upon my finger. It was a crime to win a girl's love when you had no love to give in return; it was a crime to allow you to think I would become your wife, for I loved another better than you."

"And *now*, Madge?" questioned Matthewson hoarsely; "you do not love another better than me now?"

"So *much* better!" she cried; and then seeing by the moonlight how ghastly his face was, she exclaimed, —

"Lord help us both!"

Ah, Ina, child, you will never forget how on one summer night lighted only by stars, the brook plashed and the crickets chirped, and how shrilly the wind whistled through the cedars. Will Matthewson ever cease to remember how on the evening of a later summer the moonlight poured itself down, and how the incoming tide swept the waves upon the rocks, and how the water sounded as it receded? Yours was a terrible awakening to a beautiful summer dream, Ina, child, but far away from your trysting-place a time of reckoning came. "Be not deceived. God is not mocked. Whatsoever a man soweth that shall he also reap."

CHAPTER XVI.

A FAILURE IN BUSINESS.

Nor have I money, nor commodity
To raise a present sum.

SHAKESPEARE.

Then do but say to me what I should do,
That in your knowledge may by me be done,
And I am prest into it.

SHAKESPEARE.

ON the first day of October Henry Matthewson returned to his city home with a new look on his face, and his gayety of manner all gone.

The night after his return, as he was sitting in the library with his family, he made known the fact of his broken engagement. His mother congratulated him on being free from "that girl;" but he replied quietly that the engagement was broken by Miss Munroe, and he did not consider that he was to be congratulated.

"The idea of a poor working girl refusing a descendant of the Lesters!" exclaimed Mrs.

Matthewson; but Mr. Matthewson laid his hand on his son's arm, and said, —

"I am sorry for you, my boy, heartily sorry."

"Ah," sighed Mrs. Matthewson, "I believe you are both demented."

Helen and Hortense felt it their duty to be thankful that "that disgraceful affair of Henry's terminated as it did," and wondered "what his plebeian tastes would lead him into next."

But very soon after his return home events transpired which drove the thoughts of Henry's broken engagement out of the mind of every member of the Matthewson family but himself. One of those great financial whirlwinds which uproot and shake the very foundations of business swept over the city, and hundreds of men lost the wealth they had been years accumulating. It was in vain that Mr. Matthewson labored day and night to avert the impending disaster. A week after the panic began he went one day to the beautiful house he could no longer call his own, and told his family in only half-coherent words that he was not worth a dollar in the world, and that the bank in which was deposited the money Henry had received from his uncle, had utterly failed.

The scene that followed this announcement ended in Mrs. Matthewson fainting and being carried to her room, followed by her tearful and bewildered daughters.

It was on the evening of the day on which he had brought home his unwelcome news that Mr. Matthewson stood by the drawing-room window in the gloaming and thought of things present and past.

"Heaven knows I have done my best," he said, as though some one had accused him. His mind, wandering backward, as it had often done before, dwelt on the scenes of his youth. He wondered if fate had been kind to her of the gentle face who once loved him, or if she had grown, like himself, too old for the years she had counted, and as well used to worry and care. His face was haggard, and a feeling of utter helplessness pervaded his whole being. He was in the house with wife and children, but he was utterly alone, and there is no desolation like that which comes when our own stand aloof from us and will not understand us. His wife and daughters had plainly hinted that it was their belief that his financial downfall had been due to his own mismanagement; and Henry was silent on the subject. He was one of the thousands who need the tonic of unselfish affection, of kindly, encouraging words.

The door opened, and Henry Matthewson moved across the carpet and laid his hand on his father's shoulder. His head was thrown back, and there was a defiant ring in his tone as he said, —

"We'll weather it, father. Fate sha'n't have *everything* her own way. I can work. Tell me where to begin."

How the worn and troubled face of that father lighted up! A line of poetry came to his mind, and with the substitution of two words he repeated it, —

"Strong in his children should a father be."

He became strong in an instant under his son's words, and the thought flashed into his mind if all his lost wealth could purchase manliness for his boy it was well lost.

But no sudden resolution to be more of a man had caused these words spoken to Mr. Matthewson. There was no high, generous thought that former things should be passed away and all things become new within and without. Henry thought broodingly and bitterly that life was using him too roughly; was unkind to his father, whom in a careless, neglectful way he had always loved. "Fate sha'n't have *everything* her own way," was the keynote of his thoughts. He threw down the gauntlet of defiance, and stood up looking the world in the face with the disdainful confidence of one who is ignorant of the strength of the thing with which he grapples. But Mr. Matthewson did not stop to analyze his son's feeling. He was immensely comforted in him and his resolves, and the two sat till nearly two o'clock discussing business matters and making plans for the future.

Mr. Matthewson was so cheerful the following day that his wife and daughters began to hope that his affairs were not as bad as he had feared, and many said, "Poor Matthewson!" who were not as content as the one they pitied. Henry was kind, and ready for business. This was Mr. Matthewson's stock in trade.

"More helpful than all wisdom is one draught of simple human pity that will not forsake us," says George Eliot.

CHAPTER XVII.

A BRAVE DEED.

We know not of what we are capable till the trial comes; till it comes, perhaps, in a form which makes the strong man quail, and turns the gentle woman into a heroine.

MRS. JAMESON.

WHEN Mark Winter could take each day some nourishing food, and sit for an hour or more each morning by the window propped up in his easy chair, Ina went back to Millerville. Madge had been told the good news, and could not help hoping that in spite of her sin God would some time let her be happy.

Bert received Ina literally with open arms; and Rex, who stood beside his cousin on the platform, said as he shook hands so cordially, —

"You took away and brought back much of our sunshine."

And Ina felt the preciousness of such a welcome as that.

It was a few days after her return that one

dark, stormy morning as she sat in her office-rocker reading a book Rex had brought her the night before, Bert entered slowly and with a most woe-begone expression on her face.

"Why, Berty, you look sober as an owl!" exclaimed Ina when she had bidden her friend good-morning.

Pushing her hat back in a rakish sort of way, Bert said, —

"Best beloved, you see before you the miserable and not-to-be-comforted victim of misdirected kindness!"

"Who has been inconsiderate enough to be kind to you?" asked Ina.

"Uncle Hilton," said Bert. "He was up in Grovetown the other day, and met an old friend, Prof. Greenleaf by name. This learned gentleman is going to give a party, and he has invited uncle, and made him promise to bring Rex and me. Auntie will go of course. There are to be a senator, an ex-governor, a mayor or two, and I don't know who else there. Uncle thought I'd like it, of course, and I didn't tell him I didn't want to go, for he's just as good as can be to me, and I know he dislikes terribly to break a promise unless there is some very good reason for doing it. I've been considering the advisability of spraining my ankle, or taking something to make me sick. If an accident or illness kept me away, of course uncle would be quite excusable for not bringing me."

"Why do you object to going?" asked Ina, laughing heartily.

"Because it will be poky as possible," answered Bert. "Folks will say what they don't mean, and not say what they do, and everybody will be too dignified to have a good time. To add to my horror, auntie has decided that I must wear my light silk that has a train. I have an 'inner consciousness,' or to speak with more clearness if less elegance, a feeling 'in my bones,' that that trailing abomination will drive me so near desperation that I shall take the train up and let it hang over my arm, and thus disgrace the name of Hilton. Ah, me! I wish uncle would take you instead of me. Perhaps the dress would fit you, and a train would be as becoming to you as a peacock's tail is to him. And you told me you liked to see people who were above the common walks of life, while I wouldn't give a penny to see a dozen presidents, or the Czar of Russia, or the great Quaker bitters man, or any other celebrity."

"The idea of *your* dress fitting me!" said Ina. "When is this troublesome party to be?"

"To-night, even this very night!" groaned Bert.

"But will it not be postponed on account of the storm?" said Ina. "It seems to me I never saw it rain harder."

"Oh, no," said Bert. "It seems that the senator, who is to be the bright particular star of the evening, is to go away to-morrow at noon, so the party is to be given rain or shine."

"Do you return before morning?" asked Ina.

"We come on the express that's due at Snowdon at 2.10 A.M.," said Bert. "The carriage is to be sent for us. Too bad that train don't stop here. Bless me! It's most eleven o'clock. I must go. You'll see me to-night in such attire you'll think I'm Queen Sheba's ghost."

She kissed her friend, and walked solemnly out of the office.

That evening just before the 7.15 train was due she appeared arrayed in the despised silk, and with everything that helped to make up her attire rich and immaculate.

"I suppose," she said in a resigned tone, "that I *look* nice, and I know that I *feel* dreadfully!"

Ina sought her room rather early that night. She had been kept awake the night before by neuralgia and so was drowsy and dull on this evening. She was in bed but a few minutes when she fell into a sound, dreamless sleep. It seemed to her she had slept but a few minutes when she awoke with a start, and the first thing she thought of was that a valuable watch belonging to a cousin of her boarding mistress was in her office. She had, at the request of the owner, taken it from a jeweller's where it had been repaired. When leaving the office at night she had forgotten to take it. The next thing that came to her mind was a remark she had heard the station agent make a day or two before, —

"There seems to be a general breaking into of stations along our line. Shouldn't wonder if this was the next one the rascals tried."

Suppose the station should be entered that night and that watch stolen!

She felt the perspiration start on her forehead

at this thought. "How careless of me to forget it!" she exclaimed sharply to herself. After a moment she added,—

"I will get right up and go after it."

Hastily arising, she lighted a lamp, and quickly donned her clothing. She stole noiselessly down stairs and went quietly out at the front door. The railroad was near the back of the house. By going up the track she could sooner reach the station, to which she had a key, and so she chose that way. On she went, bounding over the sleepers, until she came to where yesterday a wooden bridge had spanned an ordinary river, but now the bridge was almost entirely washed away, and the river was no longer an ordinary one. It had grown to a swollen, rushing, brawling torrent. The rain, which until twelve o'clock had fallen steadily and heavily, had now ceased, and the full moon shining through the thin clouds overhead showed her what was before her.

As she stood gazing at the flood at her feet the town clock struck one. She was much surprised at the lateness of the hour, and then the thought flashed into her mind that the night express was due in Snowdon at 2.10, and, great heaven! if it was not stopped it must go through this gap into the river. She must save those people on that train; and to do this she must have a light. Up the track an eighth of a mile away was a switchman's shanty. She turned and ran towards it with the fleetness of a deer. She found its door locked. Oh! what if she could not succeed in making an entrance! But she found a window unfastened, and opening it, fastened it up with a stick she found on the ground. She laid her palm on the sill preparatory to entering the building. Her hand touched some loose object, and, oh joy! she had in another instant discovered that it was a card of matches. With it in her hand she stepped into the shanty, and lighting a match looked around for a lantern, but found none. Back through the window and to the track she rushed, the precious matches grasped tightly in her hand under her cape. Now she must get on the other side of the river, for forty rods beyond it was a curve. If she stood where she was the engine must come around the bend before her light could be seen. Then it would be too late to brake up the train before it reached the gap. It was a perilous thing to attempt to cross that mad, swirling water on the frail remnants of that broken bridge, but not for a moment did Ina hesitate. She gathered her skirts up in her hand, saying in a low, intense tone, —

"I will not, I *must* not fail you, my friends. Bert, my girl lover, dear kindly Rex, I will lose my life if need be in trying to save yours!"

Carefully she stepped upon the structure that quivered beneath her weight. Carefully, steadily, but still quickly, for there was no time to lose, she picked her way along. Her breath came in quick, hard gasps; her every nerve was strained to its utmost tension. She made no false movements. Every step told. In some places there was only room to put one foot before the other, and the threatening water was beneath. But at last she reached the opposite shore. She made a desperate effort to keep herself from fainting, and started for the curve. When she had reached and gone around it, she removed her cape, first putting the matches in her hat, took off her dress, which was a light cambric wrapper, and replaced the cape upon her shoulders. She held the wrapper under cover that the upper part might not become damp from the mist around her.

Then, with the matches again in her hand, she stood, still and watchful, waiting to hear the rumbling of the train.

It seemed a long time to her, but in reality it was only a few minutes before she heard its distant thundering.

She knelt on one knee, and over the other bent one hung the dress, the upper part toward her right hand.

She would have made a noble subject for a painter as she knelt there with the cloudy sky above her, gazing steadily down the track, her hair, which had become loosened, falling in a heavy raven mass behind her, her hand rigidly holding a match; the dress over her knee; her whole expression denoting intense expectancy. When the rumbling sound became more audible the anxious eyes beheld away down the straight road the gleam of a headlight. Quickly a match is struck upon her woolen skirt. It lights, flickers a few seconds in the encircling fingers, and then goes out. Another is struck, and that too lights and goes out. Ah, distracting thought! They may *all* go out! Another is struck while the rushing sounds horribly near. This one burns up steadily, and is held against the upper part of the dress. The garment is thin and burns like tinder. With all the strength engendered of a great courage and a great fear she waves the blazing signal across the track. A short, sharp whistle is heard; the train slackens, and finally stands still. Ina sank on the track motionless and strengthless. When the men came forward to learn what was the trouble they found her with the smouldering remains of the dress beside her, unable to move.

"The — bridge — it is — gone," she managed to ejaculate, and then became quite speechless.

As the light of the conductor's lantern flashed over her face, Rex Hilton, who had come forward with the others, exclaimed, —

"Great heaven! it is Ina, our brave young friend!"

He took her up gently in his strong arms, arranged with care her cape about her, and rested her head on his shoulder.

"Conductor," he said, "please find my people and send them here. This young lady is a friend of ours. I will take her home."

The Hiltons were well known to the conductor, and he moved away to do Rex's bidding.

Very soon it became known to the passengers that but for the forethought and bravery of a young girl they must all have been hurled into the river whose roaring they could plainly hear, and one and all they left their seats and pressed forward to applaud and thank their deliverer. But Rex waved them back.

"She is nearly or quite insensible. I will take her home," he said.

"O Rex, tell me she is not hurt or in danger; only frightened, just frightened and weak!" cried Bert, walking by her cousin's side. And Rex answered, —

"Only frightened and weak, Bert."

"Three cheers for our preserver!" cried some one, and out on the night air rang the hearty shouts of the admiring, grateful throng. But Ina still was mute. She could not talk yet.

And Rex thought as he bore her along how pleasant it would be to care for her always.

CHAPTER XVIII.

DAYS OF HARDSHIP.

But midst the crowd, the hum, the shock of men,
To hear, to see, to feel, and to possess,
And roam along, the world's tired denizen,
With none to bless us, none whom we can bless;
Of all that flattered, followed, sought, and sued;
This is to be alone; this, this is solitude.

BYRON.

"WANTED. Ten able-bodied men to work in an iron foundry. Good wages given. Address, or apply in person to Hilton & Son, Millerville, Pa."

HENRY MATTHEWSON had been turning the morning paper over and over in a vain search for something that might meet his want of work when his eyes fell on this advertisement.

"Wonder if I could get one of these chances," he muttered. "Don't seem to be anything else for me. Pretty rough work for a fellow that never did anything harder than hold in fast horses and play base ball. I'll write to Hilton & Son. If I should apply in person, my chances, I'm afraid, wouldn't be of the best. Perhaps I should prove stronger than I look."

It was now the fourth week in October, and the Matthewsons had just moved into a small, comfortable house a half-mile out of the city. Mr. Matthewson had secured a situation as salesman in a large dry-goods establishment, and his salary was all the support his family had. Henry had tried in vain to find employment. No one of the many to whom he had applied wanted book-keeper, clerk, or salesman; or at least no one wanted *him*. Perhaps his imperious way of asking had something to do with his disappointments. He would have said, had he thought of the matter, that the declaration, "He that humbleth himself shall be exalted," was all rubbish. "The world belongs to the energetic," says some one. Matthewson's manner in these trying days seemed to proclaim that the world belonged to the educated and haughty. He was beaten but not subdued. His father's face was growing thinner and paler each day. He walked and walked, and applied at every place he came to where there was a *possibility* of employment. Most of us, either by experience or observation, know what it is to look for work;

how it wearies the brain and sickens the heart of even those who have all their lives earned their daily bread, and perhaps have gone through this experience more than once. Think then what it must have been to one quite unused to even the thought of labor; whose highest ambition had been to make life as full of pleasure as possible, and whose very soul loathed the thought of asking anything of common business men. But his father must be helped, and he himself must have a livelihood.

Work *must* be had. And so with the sneer which was becoming habitual to them on his lips, and the bitterness which was seldom absent from it now in his heart, he wrote an application for a situation in the foundry of Hilton & Son, and two days after posting the letter was informed that he could begin work at once.

Mrs. Matthewson declared in an injured tone that she never expected to see a descendant of the Lesters doing menial labor, and asked her son how he "could think of such a thing," to which question Henry sarcastically replied, —

"Of course I am going there for pleasure. Most people like a warm place in winter. It will answer for Florida."

Mr. Matthewson said, —

"Go, my boy, and do your best. No honest work is ignoble. God bless you! You are a comfort to me."

The sneer left Henry's lips, and his expression softened as he looked into his father's face. He *must* wring some good thing from fate for so good a man. He would have scorned any one's pity, but angels might have pitied him in those days. He had no God. He had not let him into his life. The one woman he loved had said him nay, and, oh, torturing thought! might now never be won, for she loved another. And poverty, with all its hated restraints, all its necessities, so new, so terrible, was upon him.

Many men whose hands were calloused by toil found hard work in that foundry, with its heavy labor, seething fires, and hot air. The moisture often stood thickly upon the brows of those who all their lives had been used to severe tasks, and shoulders which had been used to no light burdens sometimes drooped. But to Henry Matthewson, who during the twenty-six years of his life had never, before coming to that manufactory, done a real day's work, the labor was simply terrible.

He found that sinew and muscle were wanting in his arms, that necessary strength would not come at his bidding. Day after day his face paled, his thick hair became saturated, and his slim figure bent and trembled as his tender hands grappled with his weighty and unusual tasks.

A hundred times did he resolve to resign his position and go back to the city. But what could he do in the city? He might not find lighter work, perhaps no work at all; and it did not seem right to give up a place where he was receiving a good salary for an uncertainty. And so he stayed on.

The work done for Hilton & Son was necessarily hard, but all that the Hiltons could do for those serving men and their families was done. For those who were married there were pretty, well-ventilated cottages, well planned, well built, with gardens at their rear, and at very moderate rents. If there was sickness in one of those cottages its occupants received many a helpful gift from the great house on the hill, and their tenement was used without charge until better times came.

For those who boarded there was a house where plenty of wholesome food was served, clean, airy, rooms were furnished, and only a moderate price was charged for board. Had it not been for the nourishing and strengthening food which he obtained at the latter place Henry Matthewson would have broken down altogether. The days went on and on, and he labored and thought. He did not make companions of those around him.

The employees in the same building as himself were rough, uncouth men, with just education enough to enable them to read, not too correctly, the weekly newspaper that Rex Hilton had sent to each house; to sign, not over legibly, the pay-roll; to keep, not always accurately, their accounts with butcher and grocer.

They had plenty of shrewd common sense, and, for the most part, kindly hearts, these uncultured men; but their roughness of manner and speech forbade one of Henry Matthewson's fastidious nature and refined tastes from making intimates of them. He used them, however, with all due respect; and they, after a few useless attempts to make him one with themselves, let him alone, wondering what made the "dainty-lookin' chap so down in the mouth."

A dead weight of utter loneliness and almost

despair rested upon his heart. He fully realized how infinitely more solitary is one with those around him for whom he does not care, and with whom he has no thoughts or feelings in common, than when alone. A fair face and a pair of blue eyes still often came to his memory, and Madge Munroe was not forgotten.

He was more than wretched. But after a time he was surprised to find himself lingering in retrospective dreams over the hours he had spent on that old, far-away farm with Ina Ellerton.

Of all those who in his prosperity had flattered him, clung to him, called him friend, not one had shown himself friendly in his days of adversity. But it was for *him*, not his wealth or position, that the dark-eyed country girl had cared. Oh, to be again trusted as she trusted him; to be again thought true and noble and grand as he was to her on those summer days!

Madge Munroe had loved another when she became betrothed to him. This girl had poured out unstintingly for him the fresh, new wine of her affection. How easily he might have made things different. But he had been blind, blind, deplorably, criminally blind!

One day when his face was palest and his thoughts gloomiest, he looked up from his work and saw two gray eyes fixed with a kind, pitying gaze upon him. The owner of the eyes stood a little way from him, and had been speaking to another workman. She was a short, plainly dressed girl of apparently sixteen or seventeen years of age. He concluded she was the daughter of some of the men, perhaps of the one near whom she stood.

Seeing she was noticed by him, the girl came forward, and said, as she lifted the cover from a little basket on her arm, —

"I wish you would accept one of these oranges, you look so faint and tired. I'm afraid this work is too heavy for you."

She knew of no way to let the wan-faced stranger know that she thought about and was sorry for him but to offer him of her simple fruit. He took one of the large sweet oranges, and thanked her with a grace that convinced her that he was accustomed to far different society from that around him.

"Who is the child that has just left the building?" he asked of a fellow workman when the visitor had gone.

"That's the old gent's niece," the man replied. "Her name's Bertha Hilton, but they call her Bert. She says she's been sick three weeks. I've wondered why she ain't been round lately. There ain't a man here but thinks a sight of the bright, good-hearted little chick. 'N' the young boss, Rex, has been away too. It's lonesome when neither of 'em's round."

Matthewson thanked the man, and asked nothing more. That day's work did not seem as hard as the others had done to him.

CHAPTER XIX.

A LETTER: THE GOSPEL ACCORDING TO HILTON AND BEDE.

I am yours forever.

SHAKESPEARE.

I believe we cannot live better than in seeking to become better, nor more agreeably than having a clear conscience.

SOCRATES.

MILLERVILLE, PA., Nov. 23, 18—.

MY BLESSED CHILD, — Thanks, many and hearty, for your frequent letters. They have been not merely "crumbs of comfort," but whole loaves of positive joy. It was very sweet of you to be so anxious about me, but really, dear, there was no need. You will hardly need to be told that I am better. The doctor made his farewell visit a week ago. He looked rather as though he felt "done out"— as the English say — of a good job, because I *would* not have a fever of any respectable length. Susan says I "look like a rail." My knowledge of rails is so limited that I don't know whether to feel complimented or not, but as it is just as well to be comfortable when one can, I will endeavor to believe that rails are invariably handsome things. Oh, how I have wanted to see you since I have been able to be about the house! I wanted you sadly enough when I lay in bed, a burning, freezing, aching, troublesome bit of humanity, — how I do love adjectives! — but I didn't long for you as I have since my usual health and serene amiability have begun to return to me. My ills drove even the thought of you, "my one lover," partially out of my head. This morning when I was in the grain barn, where I'd been feeding the doves, I was so nearly broken-hearted because I couldn't see you, that I put my hands over my eyes, and went to sit down on a half-barrel behind me. I meant to have a real sentimental time, but bless me! the board over that half-barrel soon upset my plan, for it was terribly near the edge on the inside, and when I sat down I went *into* the barrel, and got a sharp rap on my head from the board as it *flipped up*. I sat for some time with my extremities uncomfortably near together, unable to stir, a battered and disconsolate personification of grief, till my cries brought Dennis to my relief. I put off my sentimental mood for a while, and went into the house to rub my big bump in arnica.

Rex came home last night. You can imagine how glad I am to have him back. His being called away on that stupid business the day after you left proves once more that something musty but ever-true proverb, "It never rains but it pours." I did everything I could to show my joy at his arrival; kissed him and pulled his hair, patted him and stuck pins into him, until he declared my welcome was too *pointed*, and went off to the library to read his letters. Alas! men never appreciate what we women do for them!

Isn't it glorious your uncle Mark is getting so strong again? I am so glad! It seems to me the dear mother must feel as did Martha and Mary when their brother was with them in the home again, his life given back to them and him. I should like to see that pretty, blue-eyed operator to whom you think he has given his heart. I hope she is worthy of so royal a gift as I believe his love must be. I can sympathize with him, as it was an operator who won *my* undying affection.

And now, precious, I have something so strange to tell you! It is so story-booky that I am inclined to give myself a fierce pinch to be sure I am awake when I think of it. It seems like some of the dreams that come to me when I have eaten too much plum-cake, or a quarter of a mince-pie just before going to bed.

I was down to the foundry yesterday for the first time since you went away. As I was stopping to speak to Jim Roberts, I noticed a little way from me one of the new men who have come to work lately. He was a tall, handsome fellow, with thick chestnut hair, and just such a mustache as I would have if I was a man, if I had to use a hundred dollars' worth of the article we see advertised to bring out whiskers in a month. But oh! his face was so sad and tired, and worst of all, *bitter*-looking. It said so plainly that his conditions inwardly and outwardly were unfitting; that his strength of mind and body were not equal to his tasks; that his work was too rough and hard for him, and his associates utterly uncongenial. I pitied him with all my heart, and I wanted him to know that one person in that place was sorry that he was weary and unhappy. I didn't stop to contrive to do things "decently and in order." It never occurred to me to drop my handkerchief near him so as he could restore it to me, and so give me a chance to speak to him. I'm not accomplished in the fine arts. I had some oranges in a basket I was going to take to little Lizzie Barton who is sick. Well, I walked up to my bonny unknown and offered him an orange as I would any schoolboy. He took one, and thanked me as I imagine Chesterfield might have done. I had just left the building when I met Jencks, the foreman. I described the man to whom I gave the orange, and asked his name. Judge what my astonishment must have been when Jencks said,—

"Oh, that slim chap's Henry Matthewson. The work takes hold of him dreadfully. You see, he ain't used to doing much. His father used to be a rich cove. He failed a while ago."

Ina, dear Ina, surely if there remains in your heart one trace of resentment towards this man, it will all fade out if you ever see him, and realize how low he is brought. Rex and I had a talk about him this morning, and I am sure he will not long feel friendless. I hope this won't trouble you, sweet Ina. *Everything* is best for God's own.

I'm still rather weak I'm afraid, for I feel a bit shaky about my head. I will close. The happy thought that you will soon be with me again comes very often to gladden me. Love to every member of your family, for indeed I love them all for your sake.

Now, with the same fond love in my heart, and the same wish for your happiness always, I say good-by.

Your affectionate and slab-like,

BERT.

It was the last of November, and Ina had been at Brentwood nearly a month. Henry Matthewson had been at Millerville a week before she left it, but she had not seen him, or known of his arrival. The reader will scarcely need to be told that the letter we have given was written to her by Bert while she was at the farm.

It was two days after this letter was written that Rex Hilton said to Matthewson, —

"Come up to the house to-night, will you not? I should like to show you some objects under the microscope. I brought some new things from the West."

"If you really wish it I will come with pleasure" replied Matthewson.

"Of course I wish it," said Rex. "We shall expect you by half past seven, sure."

Matthewson was much more at home in the parlor of the Hiltons than in their foundry. How the large, richly furnished room, with its fine pictures on the wall, its glowing fire, and open piano, rested him! The refined speech and intelligent conversation of the cousins — Mr. and Mrs. Hilton were away for the evening — were music to him. He lay back in his easy chair with a sigh of content that was not lost upon his entertainers; and when he asked for some music Bert played something soft and low, lingering over it for a long time, and then dashed off some sprightly bit of song in her pleasing contralto, and when she had left the piano said, —

"Now the microscope, Rex. I think Mr. Matthewson is ready for it."

They all got very much interested with the microscope, and stayed looking through it for over an hour. It was when they were becoming a little tired of it that a servant announced to Rex that Mr. Gleason was in the library and wished to see him.

"I'm sorry he came to-night," said Rex a little impatiently. "I shall have to leave you to my cousin, Matthewson," he added, "and if I'm gone some time don't blame me. This Gleason has a good deal to say usually, and is slow of speech.

He promised to come to the office at six, but I suppose was detained. He lives out of town, and goes early in the morning, or I would make him wait. He's one of our best customers, so not to be ignored, you perceive. I'll get away from him as soon as possible. Excuse me."

For a moment after Rex left the room there was silence. Looking up suddenly Bert saw that Matthewson was looking fixedly at her.

"Pardon me," he said; "I believe I was staring. I was wondering if you were ever unhappy. Your face is so full of sunshine and content, I fancy dark days and discontented longings are unknown to you. Am I right?"

The thoughtful look that so well became her came to Bert's face, and she said slowly, —

"I think I should be *wicked* to be unhappy with this home and such friends as I have."

"But I have known people to be fretful and unhappy with beautiful homes and kind friends," said Matthewson, thinking of his mother and sisters. "But I think you have some sure way of keeping happy, and that it does not come mainly from home or friends. Will you tell me about it if I am correct?"

"Ah, yes," said Bert. "I have a very sure way of keeping happy, and I will gladly tell you what it is. I keep close to the Master, and take all the good he means for me."

"And he evidently means a good deal," said Matthewson. "But many lives are filled with real care; full of anxiety about what is or may be."

"And it seems to me," was the answer, "that the owners of those lives make much of their own misery by trying to attend both to their own and God's business. Do you think the command 'Take no thought for the morrow'—no anxious care I suppose it means—was given because the morrow was not to be thought of at all? I don't. I think our Lord meant us to be thoughtful in a calm, trusting way about to-morrow, but when we had thought about it trustingly and made our plans as best we could, that we were to *leave* it as something intrusted in the hands of a Father who has all love and power.

> 'To-morrow is with God alone,
> And man has but to-day,'

says our loved Whittier. If God is looking out for the to-morrows need we be anxious about them? Why, Mr. Matthewson, he is our *Father*, and he *loves* us. Doesn't that tell it all?"

Matthewson would have smiled incredulously or sneered bitterly had almost any one else said these things; but this child was so sincere, so earnest, so evidently anxious that he should know her secret of happiness, that he could not do one or the other.

"Do you not see," he added, "that almost everything that makes life bearable is withholden from many, or, if once given, is taken away?"

"I believe the word of God," Bert answered, "and he has declared that no good thing shall be withholden from those who serve him. But there are many who slight and disobey him steadily and persistently, and still marvel that he does not shower the things they crave upon them. Perhaps the craving itself is wrong, and at any rate Christ's directions were, 'Seek first the kingdom of heaven,' and then follows the promise, 'and all things shall be added unto you.' But many want the 'all things,' and think it hard and strange that they cannot have them without any seeking of the kingdom of heaven."

"But don't this make God out as dealing with

us in a puerile way?" said Matthewson. "He keeps things away from us because we are not good, just as a mother might torment her particularly neat child by letting him wear a very dirty frock because he had soiled it playing in the mud against her commands, or when she had told him to seek a dry place before he began playing?"

"You don't understand, it seems to me," said Bert earnestly and simply. "*I* had to think a long time about it before I understood. I don't know how to tell you what I think, but I do want you to know my idea. Suppose the child *has* only one frock, and his mother, knowing this, bids him play in safe, dry places, but he plays instead in the mud. Now, does his mother keep him out of happiness, out of his 'kingdom of heaven,' or does he keep himself out? Does it not follow as a matter of course that he must suffer and be uncomfortable? It is nothing his mother has done that makes him uncomfortable and unhappy. She has not touched or spoken to him, only to say that as he has no other frock he must wear that one. She *cannot* have it different. It is not because she is angry with the child that he wears the frock. He has no other.

"God made us in his image and likeness, that is, the spiritual part of us. It couldn't have been the body, you see. The crippled and misshapen ones would make that false. He made us with God-like powers, and gave us the God-like responsibility of taking care of ourselves. He said, 'Keep yourselves unspotted from the world.' Don't play in the mud of crime, of falsehood, of littleness, or you will make these things a part of you. Behold, I make you clean, upright, honest, and *because* you are these things, *because* your frock is unsoiled, you are happy. But we disobey, and play in the mud, and not because God has punished us, or taken anything from us, but because our frock of white, which made us so comfortable and content, is befouled and full of filthiness, we are miserable. Don't you see that we must be miserable, because we ourselves have put away what made us happy? We have only one frock, any of us. God only can give us another. One life, one heart, one principle of life. If we *will* play in the mud we must have soiled and spoiled frocks, but God is in nowise to blame. 'The kingdom of heaven is within you,' says the Book; and if this isn't true I don't believe there *is* any kingdom of heaven.

What kind of a kingdom of heaven would it be that one could get from the *outside?* Don't you see that all earth, air, and heaven would combine to thwart and destroy such a kingdom? Don't you see that riches, health, friends, always propitious circumstances, blue skies and favoring breezes, and oh! so many things must be yours, to make an outside heaven for you? And don't you know, that even if you could be sure of these things for a time you could never count on having them always? And where would your kingdom be when these were gone? God must mean something good and sure and everlasting by the kingdom of heaven. And if your kingdom is to be peace, and love, and joy, and trust, don't it make it plain in an instant that all things *must* he added unto you, not as a sort of reward of merit from God, but because of what you *are;* because the natural and legitimate outcome of *being* your best is *doing* your best; the natural reward of doing your best is getting and holding the best things. *All* things that you may desire? Why, Mr. Matthewson, it seems to me that *you* yourself are everything because God made you not only with a knowledge of good and evil, but gave you *dominion* over everything; over *yourself* most of all."

Henry Matthewson, the once gay scoffer, the late cynic, looked into that earnest girlish face, and said humbly,—

"It is a new way of thinking, but it sounds sensible and true. Bertha Hilton, how would you begin a new life?"

"It seems to me," said Bert with shining eyes, "I would say, were I in your place. Now that I have seen the instability of riches, now that I have seen that we can lay no sure hold on earthly pleasure, now that I realize that whatever the kingdom may be it is *not* an outside thing, I will make a solemn covenant with God and myself to see what a real *manhood* can do for me; to put behind me all that is gross and wrong and careless, and *leave it behind me* for good; to do my *best* at all times in all things, Sundays and week days and all. I would fix it in my mind that religion 'is something else than notions,' as Adam Bede said; that it is not half so much talking as it is being and doing and becoming; not some vague, mystical, far-away thing, but a *right here* and now business. A friend of mine who hears brilliant sermons, but don't see very much result from them, calls these so-called religious essays 'literary sky-rockets.'

And a good many sermons *are* sky-rockets. There is a brilliancy that attracts about them, but there is no warmth or power in them. It is not sky-rockets that help and serve us, but the alive, glowing, warm-all-through coal, though it may be homely and anything but poetical. *I* want a religion that will keep me from letting my temper blaze as it is too apt to do; that will send Tom Smith home sober instead of drunk; that will make Sally Ryan speak gently to her children instead of abusing them; that will make the fastidious Mrs. Merrivale go into poor houses and minister to the needs of the destitute *personally*; that will fill *you*, Mr. Matthewson, with hope and courage and determination, and make you all you *can* be. This kind of religion, or none, for me!"

Before Matthewson could reply Rex came in, and soon after the visitor said good-night.

"'Something else than notions,'" was his last thought before he went to sleep that night. "Well, Miss Bertha, your sermon wasn't a literary sky-rocket" anyway. Whatever comes of this night's talk I believe in the gospel according to Hilton and Bede."

CHAPTER XX.

DAYS OF CONVALESCENCE.

How can I tell the signals and signs
By which one heart another heart divines?
How can I tell the many thousand ways
By which it keeps the secret it betrays?

LONGFELLOW.

WHEN Mark Winter was able to leave his room each day, and spend a part of the time on the piazzas or sands, his mother, with many cautionary injunctions, left him and went back to her neglected home duties. He would have accompanied her, but Dr. Vander strongly advised his staying near the sea till he was stronger, and it was not with unwillingness that he remained where he could daily see and speak a few words with Madge Munroe.

The ladies of Silver Beach chose to make a lion of Mark. They had never had among them before one who had so good a right to be called a hero, and they made the most of their present advantage. His appearance on the piazza was a signal for half a dozen to spring forward to offer him an easy chair, and for another half dozen to run towards him with foot-rests. One was afraid that "dear Mr. Winter" was sitting where the wind came too strongly upon him, while another was sure that the sun was shining too hotly in the place where his chair was placed. One wanted to raise his foot-rest, another to lower it. They brought him fruit, and sent bouquets with scented cards to his room; in fact, bored terribly the man who was so accustomed to waiting upon himself and who wondered in his simplicity what all these attentions were for. He was gracious and gentlemanly, however, to all, but discouragingly quiet. But his devoted attendants chose to call him "delightfully reticent" and "pleasingly reserved," and to shower what they considered delicate favors upon him.

There was just one woman at that favorite place that Mark cared for and gave thought to; a busy, hurried woman who found no time to bring him chairs or foot-rests, and had no fruit or flowers to offer him; who could spend only a few minutes each day in speaking to him.

His face steadily lost its pallor, his gait became

steadily surer, his stay on the piazza and sands every day became longer; and at last he went to her office window one Saturday evening and told Madge that on Monday he was going away, and asked if on Sunday she would walk with him on the beach.

The next morning came clear and warm; not too warm, for a sharp summer breeze was blowing, and the sea was throwing up its spray and dashing its waters about like a monster at play.

Before most of those who had seen fit to lionize him were out of their rooms, Mark was off with Madge for a happy time on the rocks. The two walked some distance before choosing a resting-place. They wished to be beyond the crowds that would soon be on the sands.

Apparently matters between the man and girl who sat on the large rock looking out over the waves remained as they had done for months, but in the heart of each was something that whispered that in spite of all outward seeming, things had changed. They said but little, but their silence was a contented one. Once looking at his companion and seeing her face all alight with some inward thought, Mark asked, —

"Will you tell me of what you are thinking?"

And Madge answered him with her eyes still on the waves, —

"I was thinking that 'the life *is* more than meat, and the body more than raiment.' These words come to me in a new way somehow."

He did not reply, or question her further. He understood, and it was enough.

A young exquisite, gotten up in a way that showed his tailor was a fashionable one, with a young lady apparelled with costly and fanciful care, strolled by the spot where our friends were sitting. The young man was chatting airily away, and his companion was laughing in an affected manner at his words. The former, when he had passed Mark and Madge, said, —

"That's the fellow that has been sick at the Clarendon, and the telegraph operator. I've been horribly jealous of that chap. You ladies have been so ridiculously attentive to him, you know. Don't see what you see so fascinating in the overgrown countryman."

"Ah," cried the lady simperingly, "you mustn't call him names. He *is* charmingly large, but he's losing some of the paleness that made him look so interesting. I think I'll drop him for fear he'll get to be a red-faced, burly fellow later."

"Well," said the young man, "after that speech I'm inclined to forgive him for monopolizing so much attention, especially as he seemed so serious just now. Guess he isn't having a very happy morning of it."

"And Miss Munroe was sober as a parson I should say by her looks," declared the lady.

And yet it is to be doubted if the two who with jest and laughter spoke of the couple they had passed were half as peacefully happy as were they who had called forth their light words. Holland says, —

"To the profoundly happy merriment is but a mockery. Indeed, nothing is more serious than happiness."

"I will say nothing—yet," Mark said to himself. "This day shall live in my mind — and I hope in hers — as just a perfectly *still*, peaceful one. We will not have to think that anything really *happened* at this time. And after all I may not have realized what she said that day, though, thank God, I feel that I did. But waiting is safe. I won't run the least risk of spoiling our day."

And Madge was satisfied that he spoke no word of love. It was sufficient for the present to know that the affection was in his heart.

"I will say good-by this evening if you will come out for a few minutes," Mark said as they walked toward the hotel after lingering hours on the beach. And so in the gloaming she met him again, and they walked away from the house. Again they went to the ocean's edge, and then they stood and looked at the surging water until the round moon came up and touched the waves with her glory.

"How dark it was ten minutes ago, and now how bright it is!" said Madge. "Somehow the light always *does* come, doesn't it?"

"Ay, my friend," replied Mark earnestly, "it always comes, thank Heaven, somehow."

When they again reached the house they said good-by, and Mark was gone the next morning before Madge left her room.

The summer days went on and on until all were gone. Early in September the guests began to take their departure from Silver Beach, and by the seventeenth every house was closed, and Madge went, not unwillingly, back to Brentwood.

CHAPTER XXI.

WINTER IN TWO PLACES.

> Life, believe, is not a dream,
> So dark as sages say;
> Oft a little morning rain
> Foretells a pleasant day.
>
> CHARLOTTE BRONTË.

> No life
> Can be pure in its purpose and strong in its strife
> And all life not be purer and stronger thereby.
>
> OWEN MEREDITH.

THE autumn months passed quickly and happily to Madge. She did her work with a glad, quiet heart, counting the every-day pleasures that came to her enough. Winter came all too soon; and when snow had fallen and the roads become smooth and hard, there were for her rides behind Mark's gray horse, taken in the evening or on Sunday afternoons. An invitation was occasionally given and accepted to attend a concert or an interesting lecture; for Brentwood village was a place large enough to call to it many talented people. An evening was sometimes spent at the farm; and Madge sometimes felt as though she would like this uneventful, satisfying life to go on forever.

One day in January Mark entered her office, and when he was seated drew from his pocket a paper which he unfolded and laid before her and said, —

"I have turned architect, Madge. You probably remember that I used to say that I was in hopes that some day we should build a pretty and convenient cottage on the knoll where you used to go to see the sun set. I've spoken once or twice to father and mother about it, but I never urged the matter, for I didn't want them to leave the old house unless they wished. But a few days ago father mentioned the subject to me, and said he and mother both thought we better put up the cottage in the spring. So as soon as the snow is gone and the frost out of the ground, the work will begin. We all three have been helping to plan the house. I've had mother lay out all the plan for the kitchen and pantry and dining-room. Women know more about these things than men. But I want you to look this plan over. You may see some way it can be improved. And I want you to like the cottage that is to be, for I hope that one day you will come to it to live. Will you, dear?"

"I suppose I must," she replied softly, "for I have found that I cannot get along without you."

At last they were actually betrothed. And sitting there with lowered lashes, Madge told her lover of that early home and its trials and poverty; of the often dark-browed, irritable father, the tired, broked-spirited mother, the frequently disappointed children, and of her own struggles with her love for him because he was not wealthy; and ended by saying, —

"I have concluded, however, — for oh! I have given the subject so much thought, — that father could not have had the right spirit. I am not blaming him. Never think I could do that. I do not think that he could have 'walked with God' as steadily and closely as one may walk, or his heart would have been braver, and his life less full of fretful care. I do not think you will ever grow to be like him — remember while I say this that I loved, do love him dearly — or I would never have consented to become your wife, as much as I care for you."

When she was silent he said in honest, hearty, half-homely fashion,—

"I understand you, Madge, and I don't wonder a bit that you at first refused me. But I will tell you that I don't think I will ever be exactly a poor man. The farm yields well, and in a few years I shall have a large lot of timber to sell. And, Madge, it seems to me that if I should get to be *ever* so poor I could never be anything but good and kind and patient with you, or any-one that depended on me. It just seems as though God *wouldn't let me.* I'd ask him not to, at any rate."

And then Madge took his great, strong, brown hand in both her delicate ones and kissed it.

Happy, thankful Mark, riding slowly home through the crisp winter air, smiled as Madge's words of months ago came to his mind,: "Some-how the light always *does* come."

"Matthewson," said Rex Hilton one day the last of December, "can you keep books?"

"I studied book-keeping at school," was the reply.

"Our present book-keeper," said Rex, "has

just heard of a good position near his home that he can have if he can go at once. We want to oblige him, and it will help us out nicely if you can take his place. I'm sure the work will suit you better than your present work does."

And so it came about that Matthewson left the heavy labor that had almost prostrated him, and became book-keeper for Hilton & Son, with a larger salary than he had hitherto received.

He was still thin and pale, but the hopeless, bitter look that had touched Bert's tender heart was no longer on his face. There had been no great and sudden change in him, but there had been a change. Character does not bud and blossom and bear fruit all in one season, any more than does the fig-tree. But, as atmosphere has much to do in the progress of the tree, so it does in the growth of character; and Matthewson was in a soul-growing atmosphere. He was constantly associated with Rex in a business way, and spent a good many evenings at the house on the hill. That unconscious psychology which gives the stronger and more evenly balanced mind a power over the weaker and less settled one was constantly going on, and Matthewson without half realizing it, was fast learning unspoken lessons of morality; having his old self crowded out before a new self; taking lessons in manliness in a way wholly unvoiced.

"'Something besides notions,'" he said more than once, thinking of the Hiltons and their characters. And slowly but certainly religion was becoming something besides notions to him. He never could tell just the very day and hour he was converted, but he knew that Bert Hilton's words had set his thoughts flowing in a right direction, and, as a consequence of his thinking, had come a desire to test in his own life and experience the truth of Bert's words. With this desire come the penitent cry and saving faith in the Christ. God himself could do nothing for him before it came. Righteousness, unlike greatness, cannot be thrust upon us. Sometimes it seems as though we have *too* much freedom of will.

It did not then occur to Matthewson that he had "experienced religion," and yet the work was begun and went on day after day, week after week, month after month.

We have heard heople talk of experiencing religion as though religion came like the smallpox or typhoid fever, and they "caught it" once for all; in its fulness and strength it is a slow, every-day, and for-always experience. We believe the work began with Matthewson when he first grew ashamed of his past worthlessness, and continually deepened when he lost his bitter self-conceit; when he spoke more kindly to some fellow workman; when he knelt down to ask for pardon, having decided to be strong; when his thoughts were under divine control and moving in new grooves. In short, when every experience of good intent or worthy action came, we believe he went on deepening his religious experience.

I have never seen any one who took more than the one step in any particular hour towards becoming "a new creature in Christ Jesus." Religion means not only conversion, but growing; an acclimating to God's rarefied atmosphere; a getting always near to the mount of Godliness by constant climbing, which is for the most part very commonplace and practical climbing. The religion that shows its growth *every day* is the only religion that *tells*.

Since coming to Millerville, Matthewson had heard Ina Ellerton mentioned many times. He learned that she was the special friend of Bert Hilton, and was considered a heroine, both by the company she served and by all others who knew of her noble act on the night when the bridge was swept away; but he did not meet her until after he became book-keeper for Hilton & Son. One evening in the home of the Hiltons he took by the hand a handsome, dignified, womanly girl whom Rex had introduced as Miss Ina Ellerton, but who was so unlike in manner to the impulsive, unformed, but always-charming Ina of that summer that seemed so far back in the past, that he looked earnestly into the dark eyes which he had never seen equalled, before he could be quite sure that it was the Ina Ellerton he had known that stood before him. And after all he decided that it was *not* the girl that once loved him that stood before him now.

And Ina shook hands with one who bore a familiar name, but whose grave manner and thoughtful face were not familiar to her.

Rex thought the two whom he introduced to each other were strangers, and Rex was right.

After that evening Matthewson met Ina quite frequently. They were both often at the Hiltons', and they sometimes met at entertainments. They talked together as two people who were just forming an acquaintance might have done. That summer at Brentwood was never alluded to in their conversations.

One evening Rex and Bert were in the library with Matthewson and Ina who were spending an evening with their friends.

"Did you call at Mrs. Gray's to-day?" Bert asked her cousin during a pause in the conversation.

"Yes," said Rex slowly, "and the face of her daughter Rose has haunted me ever since. It is so pale and wan and hopeless."

"Why," said Bert with interest, "when I called there last spring she was the picture of health, and was such a pretty, happy-looking girl. What has happened to her?"

"It is a duplicate of the stories we often read," said Rex. "A young man boarded there six weeks last summer, and, it seems, taught her to care for him with all her heart, and then left her without giving or asking any promises; and she has never heard from him since he went away. It seems to me some special mode of torture ought to be invented for fellows who can do that sort of thing."

"I agree with you fully," said Matthewson earnestly, looking hard into the blazing fire. "It is an ignoble, contemptible, godless thing to do. I wonder if he will ever repent truly, heartily, bitterly of his dastardly crime as does a man I know, of a similar one; if he will ever think of what he has done, as this man thinks of a like course of action, with burning regret and utter self-loathing through long days and long hours of the night when sleep would not come. I wonder if he will ever feel, as this man feels, that it would be a privilege to kneel as the sinner does to his God, and beg forgiveness of her he has injured."

Unsuspecting Rex looked wonderingly at Matthewson; but Ina, listening with downcast eyes; and Bert, looking as steadily as the speaker into the fire, knew a confession was being made, and forgiveness for a sin committed longed for.

CHAPTER XXII.

DOING PENANCE. — LONGINGS FOR NOBILITY.

We must love, and unlove, and forget, dear —
Fashion and shatter the spell,
Of how many a love in a life, dear —
Ere life learns to love once, and love well?

OWEN MEREDITH.

Better not be at all
Than not to be noble.

TENNYSON.

I DO not believe we are ever quite indifferent to one who has once loved us. Such an one never ceases to have some kind of an impression upon us. We may put such a person aside in our living, and imagine we have forgotten about the love or the giver of love. But when sunset and moonrise are meeting, when some street band or parlor instrument sends forth certain strains; when we crush some flower beneath our feet and the perfume rises to our nostrils; especially when some one we have trusted proves false to our expectations, or unequal to our demands, we remember our once-friend who loved us, and who might have been true to and sufficient for us, though we may never now speak the once often-repeated name, and vow now as always that we *have* forgotten; that we *are* free. I do not believe we are ever free, utterly and entirely, of a love that has been between us and another. It cannot vanish and leave no sign. Things that ever *were* must ever *be* in some measure and degree, and *somewhere.*

Henry Matthewson had amused himself for a summer, and left Ina Ellerton and Brentwood feeling himself master of the situation. Had he lingered he might have drifted into a stronger feeling than that of admiration for the handsome country girl; but he did not linger. She might, it is true, have been trained into something far different from what she was by the associations in his world, but there were ready-made girls enough who were handsome, and eager to show him favor. Why should he take unnecessary trouble? He had had his summer, and if he felt somewhat different towards Ina Ellerton than he had ever felt towards any other girl, the feeling would vanish when he was once away. She would forget him as he would her. All was well. The world would go on just as though that summer had never been. Fool and blind! Things can never go on after something has happened, as though nothing had happened. To declare it can is to assert that causes do not produce effects.

That Matthewson had already reaped bitter fruit from his ignominious sowing we have seen. That his crop was not yet gathered we have yet to see. In those hard, bitter days when Madge Munroe had given him back his ring, and when poverty had clasped him within her iron folds and shut him out from ease and comfort, and in with toil and misery, he thought not so much of what had been with Madge Munroe as of what might have been with Ina Ellerton. The blow dealt him by Madge's words spoken at the seaside had indeed made him most miserable, but later his thoughts did not so much continue with her who had promised to be his wife without loving him, as they went back to one who had loved him, but of whom no promise had been asked. He had learned how easily so-called friends may "begin with one accord to make excuse" when riches have gone. How light a hold one has on another whose heart does not go with his promises. He had begun to learn how uncommon a thing real unselfish love is. And the one thought that made all this hard knowledge in any way endurable was that once — it seemed so far back viewed through all that had come between — a girl had really loved him for himself. That much was true. Something was real. Ina Ellerton had been sincere.

This knowledge kept Henry Matthewson from being quite a cynic, entirely a sceptic, in those tortured, chaotic days when the earth was as iron and the heavens like brass. And now he had met Ina Ellerton again; not the unformed girl of Brentwood, not the confiding summer friend who had met him without discretion and loved him without question, but a graceful woman who was honored as a heroine, and respected as one far beyond ordinary people in point of bravery and beauty. She was, he felt sure, still one of the true kind. Her atmosphere — every one has one recognized or unrecognized — was still clear. She would love, when she loved at all, as sincerely if not as blindly as on that faded summer. She would *be* all she appeared, and more. Her love would be a royal gift, her favor more precious than "much fine gold."

In that dangerous summer Ina Ellerton had been left alone with her love to weep tears that no one saw, and to cry out in her sleep when sleep came to her; to think till brain and heart were utterly weary with thinking, and to know that nothing might come of it all. She was here now. Matthewson had met her, had confessed his sin and shame to her.

"I love her, I love her!" he cried in his chamber with his hands before his eyes. "I love her, but she is so far away from me!"

And sleep brought him visions of her, and he cried out to and about her in the darkness, and thus awoke himself, and lay thinking of her many hours.

He had met her and he loved her. What then? *Nothing* then, he told himself gloomily. The child had become a woman; a lovely and loved woman at that; and more than this, a woman who had found him out, a woman who must remember; still more, a woman with an uncle who was like a father to her, and who despised him. What hope for him in his poverty and humble estate? He went over the ground again and again, and still found no hope. More than one punishment was meted out to him for his summer's pleasure. We always gather more than we scatter. It is an inevitable consequence. But what if he could redeem himself? What if by some act or acts of nobleness he could blot out his past and enrich his present? What if he could by some superhuman effort, some self-sacrifice that could but be noticed and remembered, *force* the respect of both her and that uncle who despised him and could look so stern? Had not many a love from Desdemona's down been begun with admiration of brave deeds? But Othello, and all the rest of the fortunate lovers who had won love through admiration, had lived in times when there were opportunities for wonderful things. They did not have to wait and sigh for opportunities that might never come. He was striving to be a man now, to be sure, and the fight was steady and severe. But what did she know of his struggles? And why should his strivings to be manly be more to her than any other man's? The world had a right to demand that every one should be his best. Oh! for one grand, glorious chance to show to her and that other that he could and would be more than he *must;* to make himself worthy in their eyes, even though he might never win the love he craved! It would be worth any sacrifice to know that she respected him; that that uncle could no longer despise him.

The days went on, and still Matthewson dreamed, and awoke, and remembered, and through long hours cried out for something to do or bear that would be noble enough to make two people forget a summer of the past, and remember only his bravery.

Patience, Matthewson! Even now your chance for nobility and sacrifice is preparing. Even now those who have never seen you, or set eyes upon your star-eyed friend or the uncle who can look so stern, have prepared to give you your opportunity to prove yourself brave enough to be respected and admired by her and him.

Bert Hilton was also striving after nobility, but she did not expect to reach it by any deed especially daring, or any sacrifice especially noteworthy. In short, the word nobility did not come to Bert at all. She was simply trying to see the right way, and do the right thing. Of course this is simply what nobility is, but Bert did not name her desire thus. She had a great problem to solve, a great question to answer, and she wished the solution and the answer to be just right, and arrived at once for all. Bert was one who could never tolerate uncertains. She sifted or thought a thing down to the bottom, and then acted or rested on her decision.

"I must have this matter out," she said one day soon after she had heard Matthewson's confession. She sought her room and locked herself in. Sometimes she walked the floor, sometimes she sat down with her fingers running through her rough curls. Her face was very grave. She was every inch Bertha as she thought. After a long time she sank on her knees for a few minutes.

That evening when tea was over, and Mr. and Mrs. Hilton had gone for a drive, Bert, who was in the library alone with her cousin, drew an ottoman to his feet, and seated herself in her favorite position for confidences.

"I know you are always just and right, Rex," she said, "and so I come to you as I ever do. You know I told you when Ina Ellerton first came to Millerville that I loved her. You laughed a little at me then, cousin, and I laughed somewhat, too. But you will not laugh to-night, Rex, and I shall not either, for I am very much in earnest. It is not only true that I love Ina Ellerton, but it is *emphatically* true. I don't care anything about the theory, Rex, that one girl cannot really love another. I never shall stop to argue about the matter because I *know* that I love her. I know that to be with her is joy; that to lay my head on her shoulder and feel her hands about my face, and her kisses on my lips, is to be *utterly content, entirely happy.* To feel that she loved another better than me would be torture. But, Rex, I have had a long, sunny time in life, and if I am to have hard things, as I suppose everybody must sooner or later, I want to be able to bear them as I should, and not to be ungrateful for my beautiful past, but to do just right *every time.* I think, yes I feel sure, that Ina has another lover. (Am I leaning too heavily on your knees, dear? You seemed to tremble.) Matthewson loves her. I have watched him when with her, and noticed many things which make me certain that this is true. I have been trying so hard to determine whether it would be best for her to love Matthewson, best for her to marry him, and, Rex, I don't believe it would, at present at least. Ina was not mistaken in thinking she had a message for girls. She is writing a strong, sweet, *telling* book for them. It is nearly finished, and I have seen the manuscript. One day she will give something to others besides girls. Our girl is a writer born, Rex. I say she will give something to others besides girls. She will if she is left alone with her work; the work I am sure God meant her to do. But let her fall in love with Matthewson, and her future will be as irretrievably ruined — her future as a writer — as that of Avis was as an artist when she married Ostrandar. Understand me, Rex. I like Matthewson. He is trying to be a noble man, and is succeeding. But without meaning to be selfish, or realizing that he was doing anything but the right thing, he would absorb a sweetheart's or wife's attention. He is not patient, he is not restful. He would act on one who loved him as a constant *excitive.* Ina has too delicately poised a mechanism, too sensitive nerves, and too imaginative a brain, to wed one like him. She needs about her one who is strongly calm, steadily thoughtful; one who will take thought for her, keep her still and cheerful and comfortable, without seeming to make any effort for her; and let her work on. In a poor man's home, with a poor man's children about her, don't you see how she would put all her thought, all her vitality, all her youth and health and strength, into the work just around her, and become a prematurely old woman with her *great* work undone? I can imagine how Grant Allen and his followers would reply to this question, but I believe, and I think you will agree with me, that while it is, and always will be, the best and noblest thing for the majority of women to make and keep holy, sweet homes, to rear and send into the world strong and beautiful men and women, there is many a woman whose best work for herself and the world must be done with pen or brush in hand; with the nurse's cap or the Red Cross badge on; in lecture halls; *anywhere* where the *very best* that is in her will come out and spread itself for the benefit of humanity. Oh! I have thought it all *way down to the bottom*, Rex, and it does seem to me I am right. Ina's girl lover is patient, Rex; not very wise or strong in most things, but wise enough to know that the love that is always in readiness to serve her; that is willing to have her near or absent as is best for her and her growth; that is ever on the alert to keep her heart fed and satisfied while her brain does its best; that will come to the front or keep in the background, as is required for her interest; that leaves her time and imagination free; that will never distract her attention from the one great thing of her life, — wise enough, dear Rex, to see this, must be the kind of love she needs now; and this is the kind she claims and shall claim from me. I am strong enough to do anything she needs to have done by me; strong in my affection for her, strong in my loyalty to her. Am I right, Rex, in deciding for myself between her two lovers? Is it right for me to resolve that I will not throw her and Matthewson together any more than I can help, that I will keep her mind from him if possible? Judge between us, cousin. Forget that you love me, and tell me your honest opinion. My Father knows that I want to do *just right*."

Rex sat silent for a few minutes, and then he asked what Ina's feelings were towards Matthewson.

"She does not care for him yet I am sure," was Bert's answer.

"Give me till to-morrow to decide," answered Rex, and Bert gave him till to-morrow, or a week if he would.

What answer to your questions, Bert? You brought them to one whom you thought heart-whole and free from all love's troubles. How should you know that since the night when the brawling river was cheated of its prey, and a fainting girl was borne through the misty darkness in strong arms, a beautiful dream which was beginning to take practical shape had hung around the mind of your cousin? How should you know that three rather than two loved your friend?

No sleep in Rex's room that night, but a vigil as full of thought and strivings as had been in Bert's room the day before. In the darkness, after hours of thinking and striving, Rex arose from his pillow and earnestly said aloud, —

"Yes, Matthewson, we must both give her up, for the present at least. And by the present I mean for years, Matthewson. I am sure Bert is right. For years she must be left to and with her work. Bert will best serve her, and, through her, the world who will read her words. I have never thought her a common girl. Why should I have dreamed she would go on just in a common woman's way, having husband and family, and giving her best to them? Perhaps I could be all to her that Bert is, but I doubt it. Love between the sexes, and marriage bring so many unthought-of relations. And Bert, little Bert, really loves her, really wants her best love, and is surely as worthy of it as you or I, Matthewson. Things are all right as they are, surely all right as they are, and so they must remain — at least for years."

Going into the breakfast room the next morning Rex found Bert standing by the mantelpiece. He laid his hand on her shoulder, and said, —

"It is best as it is. You are Ina's best lover. Keep others out for her sake if you can."

CHAPTER XXIII.

AN AUTHOR'S SUCCESS. — AN UNEXPECTED FORTUNE.

> There may come a day
> Which crowns Desire with gift, and Art with truth,
> And Love with bliss, and Life with wiser youth!
>
> BAYARD TAYLOR.

> To thee and thine hereditary ever
> Remains this ample third of our fair kingdom.
>
> SHAKESPEARE.

IT was a fair May day six months after it was decided that Bert was Ina's best lover, and the two girls were at the farm.

"I want to be the first to lay my book in grandma's hands," Ina had said; and so when the fresh new copies of the lately published volume were received she immediately made preparations to visit her old home, and urged Bert to accompany her.

"I shouldn't need any coaxing to go, sweetheart," Bert said, "only I thought they might want you all to themselves, and I have you so much.

But it will be a relief to go with you, for I'm not good for much *inwardly* when you're away. I'll go right home now and begin to pack unless I can be of use to you."

Ina's face broke into a smile, and Bert understood it.

"You're thinking, I suppose," said she, "that since I've been here this morning I've broken the mucilage bottle, spilt the ink over your dress, torn up two pages of manuscript, and smashed a pane of glass, and that if I stay longer you may have to move out. But bless us! what are mucilage, and ink, and dresses, and panes of glass to one who is so happy that she feels as though she must go up in a balloon immediately, or do some other unique thing?"

Bert *was* happy; thankful too. She had read so much of the hardships of most young authors; of the waiting and discouragements and heart-sickness that the majority of them must undergo before their first books see the light. And Ina had been spared all this. She had been fortunate in her selection of a publisher, or rather, that selection had been made for her by a literary friend of Rex's who had been consulted in regard to it.

She had had the manuscript returned to her, and been obliged to make a good number of changes in it before it was considered by the publisher in the best shape to appear as a book. Many sentences which she had built with great care and elaboration were ruthlessly run through with the critical "reader's" blue pencil *because* of the care and elaboration, and she was told that these highly finished sentences had the appearance of being thrown in for mere ornamentation, and "weakened the tone of the story." The occupation of one of the characters had to be changed because the publishing house did not approve of said occupation. Several minor changes were also made. But the work was out at last, and although there were some adverse criticisms upon it, the majority of reviewers pronounced this story for girls "strong, sweet, and *telling*," as Bert had done before it was finished.

And here it was, bright and crisp and attractive-looking in its dark-green binding, and Ina and Bert were at the farm to lay a copy in Grandma Winter's lap.

"It seemed so cold and formal to send it by mail," said Ina, kneeling at Mrs. Winter's feet.

"I just wanted to bring it my own self. And with one wrinkled old hand holding the volume, and the other resting on the writer's dark hair, Grandma Winter said, while her voice trembled and her eyes moistened, —

"God has been exceedingly good to me; good in giving me such dear children; good in preserving them from death and danger, and in giving my May's child a talent that can speak to the world. Be worthy of your gift, child, always worthy of it."

How all those country people rejoiced over their author; their girl who had "made out so well," and her home-coming! And how cordially they met and entertained Bert, of whom they had heard so much!

The Winters were in their new cottage now, and all its beauties and conveniences were exhibited with pride by Grandma Winter and Madge, for Madge was Mark's wife now. She had been married a few months before this home-coming of Ina's. It was a beautiful home, a beautiful family.

"You are happy, very happy, uncle Mark?" Ina asked, looking into the face that alone might have answered her question.

And Mark answered heartily, —

"I don't know what I've ever done to deserve such happiness. 'My cup runneth over.'"

The two girls went all over the farm with Mr. Winter and Mark the next day after their arrival, listening interestedly while they were told of improvements that had been made and were to be made, of plans and hopes and expectations. When Bert returned to the house she declared if she "wasn't engaged for life as the general factotum of a literary genius she didn't know but she would take up farming."

When the two went to their room that night a flood of moonlight was pouring into the apartment. The light they had brought was extinguished, and Ina sat down on a chair near the window while Bert stood with her arm about her friend's shoulders. Both were quiet for some time, and then Bert said, —

"This has been one of the happiest days of my life, dear, and as I have stood here I have thought of one thing that could make it *the* happiest day of my life."

"And what is that one thing, little friend?" asked Ina.

Bert left Ina's side and knelt in front of her with her hands clasped together and resting on her friend's lap. Looking up into the starry eyes she said, —

"You have told me you loved me many times; but to-night I so wish I could hear you say, Bertha, I love you *the best of any one in the world.*"

Ina looked down into the upturned young face; looked long and earnestly into the tender gray eyes, and thought how much had come into her life through this friend; thought of all the patient affection, the loving thoughtfulness that for two years had stood between her and loneliness; that had brought her so much quiet, wholesome, heartsome joy; that had brought truth to her mind and joy to her heart; that was as faithful as sweet, as loyal as loving: and she took the plain little face between her two hands, and still looking steadily into the gray eyes, answered, —

"Bertha, I love you the *very best of any one in the world.*"

The head with its rough curls lowered. The little face was hidden in Ina's lap. A glad tremulous sob was heard, and Bert's voice said brokenly, —

"O Lord, dear Lord, I don't know any words that can say it all, but I'm thankful, so thankful!"

And yet a part of the world goes on saying that girls never love each other.

Over a door which led into a medium-sized hardware store which was situated in a Western city was the sign, painted on a perfectly plain ground in the plainest of letters, "Samuel Matthewson." Said Samuel was the brother of James Matthewson, Henry's father, and was known as an eccentric and unsocial old bachelor who lived over his store quite alone but for a cat and a fluffy canary.

Not oftener than once in five years did he visit the home of his brother two hundred miles away, although that brother and his children were all the near relatives he had, and it was no secret that he never wanted any one, relatives or otherwise, to visit him unless hardware was needed. James Matthewson supposed his brother's fortune would amount to some eight or ten thousand dollars, and Henry never thought it would exceed that sum.

One morning a young man who assisted in the store came to his place of business somewhat later than usual and found the door bolted. He knew Mr. Matthewson could not be away, for he was in the store late the night before, and if he had been going away he surely would have mentioned it. After waiting for half an hour, and trying every way to obtain entrance, the young man found a policeman, to whom he stated the case, and soon means were found to force an entrance to the store and the old man's rooms. When the policeman and the young man entered the hardware merchant's bedroom they found him stretched on his comfortable cot, quite dead.

In one of the spasmodic conversations which were Samuel Matthewson's nearest approach to sociability, his clerk had learned in what city James Matthewson lived and by what firm he was employed, and so he was telegraphed for, and in turn telegraphed to his son, telling him of his uncle's death, and when the funeral would take place.

When the will of Samuel Matthewson was read it was found that his property amounted to one hundred and seventy-five thousand dollars. It was learned that several lucky speculations had greatly added to his wealth. No mention was made of any one in the will but James Matthewson and his family. To his brother the deceased gave one hundred thousand dollars, to Henry fifty thousand, and to each of his brother's daughters twelve thousand five hundred dollars.

One glad thought was predominant in Matthewson's mind as he rode back towards Millerville after the funeral was over. He could make Ina comfortable now if some time she would honor him by her hand in marriage. Fifty thousand dollars was not a large sum, but it would, if well invested,—and he would ask the Hiltons how to invest it,—yield a comfortable income. And then his face clouded. Ina was far, very far away from him; farther away, it seemed to him, than she had been six months before. He did not see as much of her as formerly. The Hiltons were as kind and cordial as ever, and invited him as often to their house, but he saw Ina there only now and then. Could it be that she avoided him? But she seemed always the same when he met her. Her manner was friendly, easy, calm; too much so for what he hoped, Matthewson thought. He knew instinctively that his newly acquired fortune would make as little difference in the regard of

Ina the woman as his larger wealth had made to Ina the child, but he would be more justified in thinking of marrying now than when his salary was his sole means of support.

Again, Ina Ellerton the child had not only developed into Ina Ellerton the woman and the heroine, but into Miss Ellerton the authoress. He saw her name in many papers, and had heard more than once the opinion that the author of the lately published book was a "woman with a future." A future! Ay, and probably a future in which he would play no part; a future that would be well without him. Well, what then? He must go on hungering for her, dreaming of her by night and day, longing again and again to do something noble enough to gain her admiration. No unhappier man rode along on that swiftly moving train than Matthewson, though he had just become heir to fifty thousand dollars.

"Will fortune *never* give me my opportunity?" he mentally cried. "Must things go on always like this?"

Patience, still, Matthewson! Your chance is nearing you. Fortune, or misfortune, will throw it in your way full soon!

CHAPTER XXIV.

A WORLD OF WATERS. — NOBLE ENOUGH.

And the floods came.

BIBLE.

The gods in bounty work up storms about us,
That give mankind occasion to exert
Their hidden strength, and throw into practice
Virtues that shun the day, and lie concealed
In the smooth seasons and the calm of life.

ADDISON.

IT was in 1879 that the South Fork Hunting and Fishing Club made arrangements to give Henry Matthewson his opportunity to show Ina Ellerton that he could be nobler than he must. To be sure, this club had never heard of Henry Matthewson, or knew of his wish, but nevertheless when it bought the old reservoir at the mouth of the Conemaugh River two miles above South Fork, Pennsylvania, it was making the first move towards giving him the chance he craved. No matter that during the two years when the wall that was supposed to be strong enough to hold in check seven hundred acres of pent-up water was being built, the builders never knew of him. No matter that while these builders raised cottages around the shores of the lake they had called into being, and while the large hotel arose in the midst of their smaller habitations, they knew no one named Matthewson; they had prepared means that would provide what he had cried out for. Nor was this all. All the little streams that found their way from the cleft rocks away up in the misty Alleghanies, and gurgled and glistened down the mountain side, helped to answer Matthewson's prayer. They joined themselves together, these many rippling streams, and in concert hurried down the Appalachian valley. On and on they flow, gathering into their waters that of other streams. Mile after mile they go on, and by and by they have become a broad, dignified stream, and some one has called them a river, and given them a name. They are known now as the Conemaugh River. The mountain loneliness and fastnesses are forgotten. Left utterly and for all time is the play of the streams. They will float in an imposing manner by the towns below. But what is this? The waters that have so lately put on their new dignity, the stream wide and deep enough to be called a river and have a name, is checked in its course. The hand of man has dared to put a barrier in its way. The strength of man is pitted against the waters that have gathered their strength from the sloping hills. Which shall conquer? For eight years man holds the victory. The waters throw themselves turbulently against their granite jailer, but there is no relief for them. Day and night they repeat their charge against the rocky wall; night and day they renew again and again their onslaught, but man is victor still. The wall holds. The gay life goes on in summer around the shores of this imprisoned, impatient, artificial lake. Man is triumphant, joyous, glad. He holds the ruling power. Nature is forced to meet his demands for pleasure and enjoyment.

But all through the summer sunshine and the autumn sadness, when winter has left its banks lonely and forsaken, and when spring is telling that soon again conquering man will come to rejoice over their captivity, the waters writhe and struggle and beat against their prison walls. Eight years of restlessness, eight years of resistance, and then the waters, reinforced by the torrents which the heavy rain-clouds have poured down, gather themselves together for one stupendous effort, leap forward in a tremendous onslaught, and with a fiendish roar tear away the granite wall, and hurry with a mighty motion down the mountain side. Eighteen miles below their late prison is a prosperous town guarded on either side by steep hills. It is day, and the hum of machinery and other sounds of labor are heard. There are driving in the streets and walking on the pavements. People are talking, scheming, planning for the present and the future. It is three o'clock, and everything is as usual at Johnstown. Everything? Not quite everything. Above all the sounds of the town there can be distinguished a dull, rushing, rumbling noise, far up among the hills. The more timid pause in their work or enjoyment every few seconds to listen to the sound, and wonder with apprehensive faces what it can be. The careless listen for once or twice, decide the noise is something that will soon cease and is nothing to them, and work away with singing or whistling lips, or are silently happy or troubled.

But listen! A report is going around that warning has been given through the telegraph office that the big reservoir is surely giving way. But the people who hear this for the most part shrug their shoulders and smile. They have heard the report many times before. Familiarity has bred contempt. They go on with their usual avocations, the apprehensive ones taking courage from their incredulous neighbors. But listen again! there is a sound of a horse galloping at terrific speed through the Johnstown streets, and a man's voice is heard exclaiming,—

"Run for your lives! Run to the hills! The dam is bursting!"

And now the timid are restrained no longer, and hundreds rush up the hillside. But the incredulous stare at the wild-looking man on his bay steed, and think him a madman, and his words of warning a maniac's cry.

But there is not much time for conjecture now. Following closely after this rider is a wall of water forty feet high. On they come, the mighty rushing waters, made mad and furious by their long confinement. They sweep through the broad streets bearing large manufactories and solid and costly dwellings as lightly on their crest as their own foam is borne. They fill the alleys and by-ways, and catching up the small shops and poorer houses carry them along like straws.

And see! Here is a sight to make the stoniest heart soft! In this relentless flood hundreds of human beings are borne along, holding up hands for help that can only reach a few, pitiably few, of them; crying out for succor that can be granted to only now and then one of their hapless number; praying to a God that seems very far off, or as their only refuge. There are gray-haired and middle-aged men, old and middle-aged women, young men and maidens, boys and girls, and little children, in this frightful maelstrom. These free, heaped-up, terrible waters are fiendish, irresistible. It was man who confined them; it is man who shall suffer. Johnstown, with its habitations, with its lives and means of living, is going out on the flood!

Two girls are standing on the bank; two girls among many other girls. They have but lately joined the panic-stricken group who are saved but "scarcely saved," and who in the terrible twilight must see friends and neighbors—and all became friends and neighbors in that time of havoc and terror—floating by with cries and prayers, or dumb with despair, or hoping even yet, calm and quiet because of their trust in One who is all-powerful.

These girls, accompanied by a man, have come in on the Baltimore and Ohio Railroad train which has been stopped near Johnstown by the flood. The one is tall and graceful, and her handsome eyes are shining very brightly as she looks out over the waste of water and its terrible burdens. The other is short and small, and her gray eyes have grown almost black as they behold the frightful panorama. Both girls have for some time been watching a man in a small boat which is being guided with consummate skill among the multitudes of floating objects about it. He has already rowed out five times into the swirling, eddying, dangerous currents, and brought to the shore people who had been floating by on pieces of broken buildings. His heroism has again and again called out the shouts of those on shore. He has rowed out again, and the girls press nearer to the water's edge that they may watch him, for the light is growing dim. And there is another person they wish to keep in sight. Their companion on the train is down very near the water trying to devise means of saving some of those praying, crying, despairing, hoping ones. They have both men in sight, and now something happens to each that draws a cry of distress from more lips than theirs. The man in the boat is knocked into the water by a floating timber, and the man on the shore has involuntarily started forward as though to rescue the brave rescuer, and is sucked into the water and swept out from land. Starry dark eyes look into brilliant gray ones, and Ina Ellerton's voice says, —

"That is uncle Mark. O Bert, Bert!"

The girls follow along the side of the flood trying to keep one form in sight among all those other forms, trying to distinguish Mark Winter from a hundred other people about him. And see! Some one has thrown a rope.

"Lord help us to save him! He's saved too many others to be drowned himself!" The thrower of the rope is thinking of the man who was in the little boat. With a gratified "Ah!" the men on shore see the rope fall near the hero. He will grasp it! He will be saved! But what means this? Is the hero determined to die that others may live? Who is this struggling near him, trying to swim, but finding swimming impossible in that turbulent, wreck-bestrewn water? Is this a fancy? Is his brain turning amid these terrible scenes, or has death come to him, and is this a face seen in the new world so like a face in the old? If his brain is not playing him tricks, if he is not dead, this is Mark Winter who once saved him from drowning, whom he will save now from the same fate. He grasps the rope, and before Mark can divine the intentions of the man near him, it is fastened about his waist, and Matthewson has given the men on shore a motion to pull away. But Mark realizes what is being done. A man is giving up his own life for his. It must not be. He gripes the man with a tremendous hold, and tries to unfasten the rope, but it does not yield to his one-handed efforts. Still with a vise-like clutch he holds to Matthewson. There is a steady, sturdy, many-handed pull from the shore, and ere long a shout of exultation goes up from many throats, for both men are saved.

Matthewson on his return from his uncle's funeral, has come into Johnstown on the Pennsylvania Railroad, and the train has been stopped by the flood.

Mark Winter had been persuaded to accompany

Ina and Bert back to Millerville when their delightful May visit at the farm had been completed.

The girls saw it all, the struggle, the double rescue. As soon as they were on shore the two men started to their feet. Mark stood up steadily, but Matthewson staggered, and would have fallen but for sustaining arms that received his sinking form and laid it gently down.

The girls had recognized the hero. They looked hard into each other's faces, and said in the same awe-struck tone, —

"It is Matthewson."

Mark knelt beside him, and placed some court-plaster, which he had found in the pocket of his coat, over a wound in the forehead just underneath the hair. A dozen people were offering dry clothing for the two men. A good number had left their homes at the first alarm, and brought articles of clothing and household furniture with them to the hills.

"Let us make him comfortable. I can wait," said Mark, as he began to strip off Matthewson's drenched garments. Willing hands assisted him and soon Matthewson was dryly clad.

A woman touched Mark's shoulder.

"We have made him a place to lie down up here a little way out of the crowd," she said. "I brought considerable bedding with me."

"Can you walk? We want to take you to a better resting-place," said Mark.

Matthewson tried to rise, but sank back, and the next instant four pairs of stout arms were beneath him and he was borne lightly and swiftly along to his improvised couch.

It is night in the Conemaugh Valley. And such a night! The flood is still rushing on, bearing its horrible burdens. Down below the town a short distance is the iron bridge built across the river by the Pennsylvania Railroad. This bridge stands firm against the onslaughts of the flood, fatally firm. Against its foundations are piled closely, compactly, the lumber that has come down the river, the wreckage of houses, many corpses, and worst of all, in this mass of timber and dead bodies are wedged many living people who are doomed to die by fire and water alike, for the mass is on fire. O God! what sights and sounds are those that fill these hours of darkness! No pen can describe them, no language give utterance to the truth concerning them.

But amidst the terrible din, while timbers are breaking against the iron foundations of the bridge with a sound like that of artillery, while the shrieks of the suffering and dying come echoing up the hillside, while hundreds of nameless noises float around him, Matthewson seems at peace, and wholly unmindful of them all. Mark has sent a man on horseback to the nearest town for a physician, and to despatch to Rex Hilton. That the doctor cannot arrive too soon the three watchers plainly see. There is trouble here that they do not understand. Matthewson is seriously ill. He seems to have lost consciousness of his surroundings. He evidently comprehends nothing about him, for he smiles and talks of roses and the summer sea.

"How do you feel now?" said Mark, bending over him. "O my noble fellow, how I honor you!"

Matthewson looked up quickly into Mark's face, looked long and earnestly. The word *noble* had caught and chained his wandering thoughts. His mind seemed to clear for a moment, and he realized something he had not thought of before. Down in that boiling caldron which he remembered now, down there where life was being sacrificed so ruthlessly to avenge the anger of the water-god, it had never occurred to him that his prayer for nobility was being answered; that here was his chance to be noble enough. He had only thought of saving life; precious human life; of doing what little he could where so much was needed to be done. But now the fact came to him that his prayer had been answered, and that she, Ina the beloved, and the uncle whose face could be so stern, but was so tender now, had been there to see him struggle with the waves for life, precious human life. And the cry went out from his heart, —

"Since this must come, I thank thee, Lord, that I was here, that *they* were here!"

His mind wanders again, but does not lose the word noble, or wholly lose the train of thought it has suggested. Brandy has been found, and is often administered in small quantities. Oh that the physician would come!

Matthewson roused from a half stupor and looked into Ina's face which was bending over him.

"Noble enough for *her?*" he whispered eagerly,

half raising his head. "Does *she* think me noble enough?"

Ina did not know what he meant. Here was some fancy of his sick brain. But she answered him unhesitatingly, using involuntarily a name that had not been on her lips for years.

"Yes, Harry, we all think you noble. You are noble enough for *her*, for any one. Try to rest now, won't you?"

"Harry," he said as he sank back on his pillow. "Harry. Who used to call me Harry? It was Ina, surely. And I am noble enough for *her!* They *all* think so!"

The physician came as morning was breaking, came and told them that a blood vessel had been broken. His coming brought no relief, no hope. Matthewson was not only deaf to the sound of the valley, but to all earthly sounds. He was one of the victims of those long-caged-up waters. He had given his life to save other lives. His prayer was answered. He was noble enough.

CHAPTER XXV.

BEREAVEMENT AND FOREBODINGS.

> He reaps the bearded grain at a breath,
> And the flowers that grow between.

> And if at times beside the evening fire,
> You see my face among the other faces,
> Let it not be regarded as a ghost
> That haunts your house, but as a guest that loves you,
> Nay, even as one of your own family,
> Without whose presence there were something wanting.
>
> LONGFELLOW.

SEVERAL of those who had been made home-less by the Johnstown disaster had found shelter and warm hospitality at the house on the hill. The bright June days which followed directly upon that night of devastation and horror were full of work and care for Bert Hilton. Her special charge was a young girl sick with typhoid fever. This girl, in a convalescent state, was among those who escaped to the hills before the oncoming of the flood. The fright and exposure, and later the ride of twenty-five miles to Millerville in the carriage which Rex had brought to Johnstown, where he arrived in response to Mark Winter's telegram, had all conspired to bring on a relapse, and she was now extremely ill. Bert tended her as devotedly as a sister could have done, giving a large part of her time day and night to ministration, earning thereby, not only the love and gratitude of the sweet young thing, but also that of her delicate, useless little mother, who hung on her words and believed in her skill and ability as firmly as though she had been sixty instead of nineteen.

All that had been left of Matthewson had been sadly sent away to his family. His three friends in Millerville could hardly realize that he had gone from them forever, and they missed him sorely, even in the midst of so many absorbing interests and cares. Their eyes shone through their tears, and their voices took on a proud ring, as they spoke of all he had done when Johnstown was going out on the flood. Surely, if he was with them in spirit, he must at last have been satisfied with the regard in which he was held.

"'Greater love hath no man than this, that he lay down his life for his friend,'" quoted Rex more than once. The Hiltons had since a certain wild night called Ina their heroine, and now all three of his friends called Matthewson "our hero."

Did you know the truth, Matthewson? Did you realize how fully and surely you were felt to be noble enough?

Mark Winter had returned to Brentwood after a few days at Millerville, and his voice grew husky, and Madge's eyes grew wet, as the story of Matthewson's nobleness was told at the farm.

The best medical skill that could be produced could not save the life of the sweet young girl. She had no strength with which to combat disease, and one day slipped out of life so suddenly and painlessly that those who watched by her side thought for some time after she had passed from the death of the body to the fuller life of the spirit, that she was asleep.

The frail body was sent away for burial, the little mother going on the same train with it, silent, stunned, wondering how such a thing *could* happen to her; alive to only one thought and conviction, — that Bert Hilton was of such stuff as angels are made of, and that nothing could ever wipe out her obligations to her.

A few days after the departure of the dead and the living, Bert and Ina sat one evening in the former's room. It was after office hours, and Ina had come to see her friend. The moonlight lay about them as it had done on that night at the farm. No other light was in the room. Again Ina looked down into the upturned gray eyes, for Bert was kneeling now, as she knelt in that other moonlight, at her feet, and the small hands clasped the whiter and more beautiful ones in a loving grasp.

"This has been a strange kind of day to me," said Bert. "A sort of hushed stillness has been about me, and I have repeated, or had it repeated to me, I cannot tell which, many times the opening lines of that beautiful hymn of Phœbe Cary's: —

> 'One sweetly solemn thought
> Comes to me o'er and o'er:
> I am nearer my home to-day
> Than I have been before.'

"Don't start and tremble, dear. You know we have been through enough lately to make any one serious. Perhaps all this is reaction. I don't wish to frighten you, darling, but you know if I should have the fever (I know auntie is afraid I shall, for I have had considerable pain in my head and limbs to-day, though I *wouldn't* give up and go to bed), it *might* be, only *might* be, you know, love, that our good times here would be over, and you will let me say a few words that won't do any harm, even if things are bright and cheerful and chipper, as they probably will be soon. If I don't stay with you, I don't want you to think of me as having nothing more to do with you or your life concerns. I feel that up there with the dear Lord I should be allowed to watch over and help you, and I know that no distance could be so great, or any eternity so long, that I should stop loving you. Always take the good that comes to you, dear. And I feel that somehow a great good is near you. One of my unnatural feelings to-day has been a conviction about some things in the future."

"Bert, dear, how strange you are!" said Ina in a troubled tone. "Surely it *is* reaction from the terrible strain under which you have been living. You should not have worked so hard and slept so little. It ought not to have been allowed."

"But I *insisted* upon doing it," said Bert. "Alice liked best to have me with her, and I was glad to put in a bit of good solid work for humanity, for, like Tennyson's Maud, I

'Have fed on the roses, and lain in the lilies of life.'

"But we won't be dismal any more. Talk to me about yourself. What are you writing, thinking, hoping? I have not seen half enough of you lately."

But Ina could not speak much of indifferent things. A heavy foreboding filled her heart, and there were very long silences between the two to whom a separation had been suggested.

When the nine o'clock bells rang Ina arose to go.

"Good-night, my wee girl lover," she said. "Get the blue fancies out of your tired head, and be sure you do something for the aches and pains to-night. Sleep well, my friend of friends."

"Good-night, precious; and O my darling, God bless you *always!*" was Bert's earnest reply.

Impulsively Ina held out her arms, and Bert's

curly head rested on her shoulder. Both felt instinctively that this was no common parting.

And the moonlight spread itself around them like a garment of silver, and the night was beautiful about them as they stood in each other's arms.

CHAPTER XXVI.

RENUNCIATION.—BACK FROM THE DEPTHS.

He prayeth best who loveth best.

COLERIDGE.

My dust would hear her and beat
Had I lain for a century dead.

TENNYSON.

IT was half an hour before sunset. All day they had watched beside her, waiting for the end which the physician said would come before midnight. She was partially conscious at intervals, but lay for the most part in a deep sleep. She had once or twice during the day smiled on them, but even this, in her utter exhaustion, seemed too much. Once in the forenoon she had essayed to lift her hand to Ina, but her strength was not sufficient even to make the effort noticed. All pain had left her, and her quietness was like that of death. Over her pillow lay the hair, which had lost its bushy look and become soft rings. The gray eyes seldom unclosed.

There were flowers all about the room. Not a child in the village but loved the girl in the great house who was said to be dying; not one but brought some offering to her sick-room. One little mite of five brought her kitten, a small, frightened, gray animal, saying, "Berty used to play with him. I thought p'raps she'd like to have him now," and turned away with trembling lips when told that her friend was too ill to notice her pet. But the lips ceased to tremble when she was told she might bring some flowers, and the next day she appeared with her tiny hands full of violets, and Bert knew from whom they came, and sent the little one (who could not be admitted on account of the contagious fever) thanks and a kiss. When it became known among the children that they could bring flowers, day after day they came with their blossoms. Sometimes it was a flower plucked from some house plant, but oftener it was some sweet wild thing such as the bringer had often gathered in the company of her whom they wished to please.

"She loved daisies, Berty did," said one little girl with a great sob, letting her apronful of white and yellow flowers fall on the carpet as she covered her eyes with her small brown hands.

There seemed to be a hush through all the place and in every home, for Bert was the child of the village. Men involuntarily uncovered their heads as they asked for news of "the little one," and women spoke softly of the "sweet little creature," and wiped away many a tear as they spoke.

And now near this sunset which should end the last day of this prized young life, Rex leads his mother out of the sick-room and insists that she shall take a few minutes' rest. Mr. Hilton is already lying down. "Rest for a few minutes, yourself, Rex," said Ina. "You look terribly tired. I will speak to you if there is the least change."

"Thank you," Rex answers, as he puts his mother's arm through his own. But there is no rest for him. When he has placed his mother on her bed and arranged her pillows comfortably, he enters the library and shuts the door. He goes to the window and looks out towards all that glory in the west, but sees nothing of it. He is thinking of those two girls, the one in her mortal weakness, the other in her great sorrow.

Day after day he has seen Ina hang over that

couch. Night after night he has seen her leave it for only the briefest time in which she could get the sleep that she *must* have to bear her self-imposed vigil. He has seen her force down the food that nearly choked her that her strength might not fail. He has seen the look of anguish come again and again to her face when Bert's eyes were closed. He knows that when life shall go out for Bert, Ina's life will be a broken and shattered existence. He knows as well as Bert has known that girls can love each other. He clasps his hands and rests them upon the window frame before him, and his head goes down upon them. The lingering rays of the setting sun fall softly upon his hair like a halo.

Rex Hilton is praying in short ejaculatory phrases, with pauses between.

"O Lord, is there *need* of another life in heaven?" he cried. "If so, take mine, I implore thee!"

And then he was tempted of the devil. We all are at times. No matter what the devil is to us, we feel the devil-influence sharp, strong, and severe sometimes, all of us. There is a time, perhaps *times*, in every life when thoughts that are strangers to its usual thoughts, suggestions utterly out of keeping with all else concerning it, temptations entirely different from any usual temptations, come as that power, whatever it may have been, came when according to Bible writers Christ "went up into a high mountain to be tempted of the devil."

"Why pray for Bert's recovery?" this something whispered. "Ina will not turn to you while she lives. If she dies you will be all that is left Ina. She will learn to love you then."

Rex takes his arms from the window frame and looks around into the solitary room with a bewildered air. Can it be *himself* that has had such a thought? *his* mind that has conceived such an idea? Facing the empty room, and raising his hand with an angry gesture, he cries in a ringing voice,—

"How dare you! Has it come to this that you are not afraid to approach me with your craven questions and dastardly suggestions? Do you think I would harbor the thought that I was *fit* for her love if I could be willing that so sweet and beautiful a life should go out that this love might be given me? Away with you, coward, traitor, *devil!*"

Whatever it is that tempts him, Rex Hilton calls it devil. We do not stop to be metaphysical when we are very much in earnest.

"I have said for years," he goes on, speaking still into the empty room, "but now I say I will hope for nothing from her *forever.* To atone for being so despicable that you could come to me, I say I will throw aside all thoughts of her save those a brother might think. Hear me, and *begone!*"

And yet Rex Hilton was not to blame for that thought any more than our Lord was to blame when he was tempted by the thought of great earthly riches and power; any more than you, my true-hearted reader, are to blame when principalities and powers suggest to you that which you loathe. The suggestion of evil, the unrighteous thought, come from whence, or whom?

Rex turns to the window again, and now his prayer goes on earnestly, continuously, unbrokenly. He cannot lay his case rapidly and strongly enough before Him in whose hands are the issues of life and death.

"Not at her hands, but at mine, take the sacrifice," he cries. "I give myself unto thee *utterly.*

Send me where thou wilt, give me any work however hard, or wherever in thy world it may be, or let me die! I ask nothing for myself. I give up all plans and hopes; but let this life be spared for *her* sake, for the sake of all who love the child! *Nothing* for me, *all* for them. Only this one thing, Lord! Let these two be happy, and *together!*"

Who shall tell us by what means prayer does its work? who explain what forces are set in motion by earnest desire and mighty pleading?

"He that will lose his life shall find it."

The giving of all that others might gain all. The laying down of all that others might lay down nothing. The abandonment of self that others might not abandon aught.

The love and the promise of the Father; the utter fulfilment in spirit of the law by the child. The positive and negative poles of the battery generating the conditions which shall make answer to prayer possible.

Ina, her very soul apathetic with grief, has been kneeling beside the bed. Beneath the burden laid upon her, her heart is numb, her very limbs seem to be paralyzed. The earth and all that therein is are naught to her. Nothing will ever matter again. Bert is dying.

After a time she raises her head and listens as though to some message. She stands upon her feet, and her heart grows strong, while a clear perception and definite purpose take possession of her mind. Just one thought possesses her. *Bert must come out of this lethargy, out of this deadening sleep.* She takes the cold hands in her own, and bends over the face on the pillow. She gathers all her strength into one place for one purpose. In full, vibrant tones she speaks to her friend,—

"Bertha, *awake!* You are coming back to life. *God is here.* Prayer has been heard. His life is here. It is for you to receive it."

Bert's eyes unclose. The torpid brain takes on an impression of life. A new feeling is born within. The brain is growing dull again, but Ina cries out,—

"*Bertha, you must not sleep!*"

It is the voice of Ina, Ina whom she loves.

An hour goes by, and the stupor is not allowed to return. Rex enters the room. Ina turns to him with a new light in her face, and Bert's voice says weakly,—

"Rex, I have been a long time asleep. It is so dark I can hardly see you."

Rex's eyes seek Ina's face, and plainly ask, —

"Is she dying?"

"Ah, no, this is life, surely is," was the answer to this mute inquiry.

All through the night Bert lay fighting a hard battle. She must not sleep. She must not yield to weakness, which meant death. She had heard the call to life. No more sleep, no more weakness, no more drawing near to death.

The divine love working through human love. The saving, mighty force sent through familiar channels that nothing might jar or seem amiss. The unusual made to seem usual. The water made wine, the bread multiplied and remultiplied, the weakness turned to strength, the wonder wrought without observation. Unfamiliar things performed through familiar agencies. The prayer answered by seemingly natural means. He spares us the shock of miracles performed in startling ways, and the scoffer cries out in his foolishness that no miracle has been performed, no prayer answered.

CHAPTER XXVII.

FACING THE OLD WORLD. — HOPE AND PEACE.

> Farewell! a word that must be, and hath been —
> A sound that makes us linger; yet — farewell.
>
> BYRON.

> Ah, well for us all some sweet hope lies
> Deeply buried from human eyes.
>
> WHITTIER.

A SKY perfectly clear save for a few white clouds toward the west. A fresh breeze stirring, the sunshine glinting on the waves. A lovely morning for the sailing of the Alhambra. She is nearly ready to pull in her gang plank. Her black smoke-stacks stand up grim and tall against the sky. She looks a mighty thing amid the small craft around her. On deck are her passengers waving every sort of handkerchief to every sort of friend on the wharf, and shouting parting messages. Among them stand two girls in blue flannel suits and sailor hats, the one tall and dark and handsome, the other short and pale, with tender gray eyes, and hair in soft, short rings.

Rex has said good-by and gone on shore. They keep him in sight as long as possible. When they have moved away from the wharf, and are a long way off, they try to find him through a glass, but he has disappeared, and the girls turn their faces away from the land with a sigh half of pleasure, half of pain. What will the Old World bring them? What will be the changes in the land of their birth and their love before they set foot upon its shores again?

Bert had come up slowly from death to life; had struggled long before her grasp on strength became in any degree a firm one. Even when she was able to go about the house and the village the old color did not return to her cheeks or the old elasticity to her limbs. She dragged wearily about week after week until Rex sought her physician in desperation, and demanded that something be done for her.

"Send her to Europe," said the doctor. "I meant to have spoken of it the first time I saw you. Send her along right off before the fall storms begin. Let Miss Ellerton go with her if you can arrange it. Wonderful girl that Miss Ellerton. Bert wouldn't be happy without her anyway, and she mustn't be allowed to fret. Strange case about those two girls. I don't understand it. Send Bertha to Europe with Miss Ellerton, and I'll warrant she'll come back gay as a lark and strong as a young pony."

"We should have to get some one else to go with her, if indeed we could induce her to go at all without you," said Rex when Ina had demurred about going to Europe at the expense of the Hiltons. "Mother is too delicate to go, and father is shut up with rheumatism, so I cannot leave home."

And then he added the words which decided the matter at once, —

"It is the only chance I can see for Bert to regain her health; and if she went with a stranger I am not at all certain of the voyage or her sojourn in Europe doing her any good. The Bruces are going over on the Alhambra the third of September. You could go in their care."

Ina paid no heed to the concluding remark. No matter who was going, Bert must go, and she must go with her. It was the only chance Rex could see for her girl lover to regain her health. Ina's mind was made up. And since she could go so rightly, since the rare privilege of which she had so often dreamed, but for which she had not dared more than faintly to hope, had been given her, not merely as a pleasure, but as a sacred duty, how glad and thankful she was that she could go.

Far out on the water, which was losing its green tint and becoming blue, Bert nestled to Ina's side and whispered, —

"Thank Heaven we are happy and together."

Happy and together. It was what Rex had prayed for; Rex's very words in that empty room; Rex who was on the train speeding away towards Millerville. Gone for a year by his earnest wish and according to his planning, but taking the best part of his heart with them. And yet he is at peace; at peace because he has given up all hope of gaining more than a brother's place in Ina's heart, and is resting and building on no uncertainties. He thinks so, and yet — and yet —

Well, Ina is very friendly and sweet and pleasant. "Just like one of our own family," say Mr. and Mrs. Hilton, and their tones have become even more cordial since those terrible days when Bert declares she was just over the borders of death and was prayed back to life.

Ay, like one of their own family, loving them perhaps even more, certainly not less, than as though she was of their blood; and although he tells himself he claims, shall ever claim, only a brother's place in her regard, Rex is glad Ina is not of their blood. Showing her regard for him in so many ways, being so interested in all that interests him, asking and taking his advice in so many matters; respecting and caring for him as she does for no other friend save Bert, — well if that other love cannot be his, this is very pleasant, and there are a good number of years ahead. And — ah, Rex, you meant all you said in that empty room. You are no turncoat. But nevertheless you are not quite correct as to the names of all your sensations, not quite honest with yourself.

The day goes on, and the night comes down. The girls watch the sunset from the deck of the Alhambra, and talk of home, and of that world toward which they are sailing. It is growing dark, and as Ina draws the shawl more closely about her companion's shoulders, she says fondly and gladly, —

"It is nice above all telling to be here with

you, little one." And Bert, with an upward look full of contentment, whispers softly, —

"Happy and together."

When at Millerville the sun goes down, and the twilight deepens into night, a man whose heart is with those two on the steamer's deck goes up the walk to the great house, lonely, but not cast down, feeding on memories of happy days that have been, and his hopes for happy days to come.

The night has come on sea and land, and Ina and Bert are happy and together, and Rex is at peace.

CHAPTER XXVIII.

GOD'S HAPPENINGS.

As we live the life and do the errands of the Kingdom in ever such weak or little ways, we find out more and more that we are set to work in the unseen. . . . He shows us a directer and solemner dealing than by mere act or word or circumstance. . . . He gives us something of his own closeness to apprehend by; to love and serve by.

MRS. WHITNEY.

"IT cannot have just *happened* that you and not somebody who would have made a stiff, hateful, *unhomable* place where we might have felt we *ought* to stay, and been just certain we *didn't want* to, were sent to us, can it, Miss Hilton?"

Miss Hilton did not answer at once, but this girl with her questions which came of deep thinking, her italicized words born of italicized thoughts, her original expressions, was not surprised or impatient. She was accustomed to her friend's pauses before her replies.

"I think," said Bert slowly, after a little, "that it was one of *God's* happenings, which are God's plannings blossomed out into *wholeness*. I don't believe he has any waste basket, but I think his piece bag is immense, and into it he puts all the fragments of lives, the things which are thrown off from lives, and put by and left behind, and all the time he is putting in his hand and taking out the pieces which have a correspondence and relation to each other, a potential wholeness in them; which fit together till some entire thing is made. We understand that there is no waste in nature; I don't believe there is any waste in human nature, in lives. I believe everything which is thrown *off* or *out* of a human heart or life, as plants shed their leaves and throw out their gases, whether good or bad, gets thrown *on* or *in* somewhere, sometime. It goes into God's piece bag to await its use, its fitting in. We cannot see the gathering up or putting together; we only see the finished thing, and so we talk of happenings."

"Yes," said the young girl, speaking as slowly as Bert had done, "I think I get your meaning—*partly* anyway, but I wonder what God had in his piece bag which *could* have blossomed into anything so beautiful as your coming."

The soft brown eyes which were once a mother's

pride, and later had had to do with their owner's almost ruin, looked into Bert's face, and the latter bent and kissed the girlish cheek before she said, —

"I can only trace part of the piecing, dear. We never can see the whole of a thing. There is a visible and an invisible to everything. There was, a number of years ago, a man who did wrong, a girl who was disobedient. One *acted* love, the other felt an affection which, had she been true to herelf and those who best loved her, would not have been kindled. Both suffered, both repented, both did penance, as all wrong-doers must whether they accept the fact and the penance or not, both sent a call towards the light, both struggled after the call nearer to the light. And hearts which had dwelt in the light were yearning toward those in the darkness, and the owners of the hearts came face to face with the need and longing of those who had eaten husks and for a while called them bread, but now were sore pressed and faint and hungry.

"The girl who had stepped out of the sunlight, who had snatched a pleasure short-lived and unlawful, and terrible in its fruits to her, became so dear and precious to your friend that she wondered that life could ever have seemed full without her. God was getting his pieces ready to put together. As time went on the thought that thousands of other girls were probably in a darkness which, if there was no one lovingly to meet them face to face and draw them back when they called towards the light, would swallow them up and make them stumble into blacker darkness, came, and stayed, and grew larger, and then was born the thought, followed by the plan, for a home for such as these. The plan was followed by the home itself, and, unworthy as I am, I am here, your friend, the friend of all our dear girls. God has put the pieces together. Even the fragments of falsehood and deceit and disobedience he has gathered up, and with the pieces of sorrow and repentance and love and good will has made something you call beautiful."

"I *do* call it beautiful indeed," said she of the brown eyes, "and if you call my friend of friends, Bertha Hilton, 'unworthy' again, remember you are insulting *me*."

Bert's eyes were full of happy tears, but she only said, as she passed her hand over the hair of the speaker: "I am going to Millerville for a few days, Brownie. I shall be off early in the morning. You will practise faithfully, and play that troublesome Italian piece correctly for me when I return, I know. Now kiss me, and run away."

It was five years since that outgoing steamer had borne Ina and Bert away from America's shores, and left Rex lonely but at peace; five years since they had turned from trying to single out their friend in the crowd, and had found themselves leaving the New World, facing the Old, happy and together.

A great deal had been in those five years. Not so much of which there were any outward signs, not so many days on which one could look back and mark it as a time on which something special had occurred, but many inward happenings, much growing up to and into the largeness of life, much solidifying of thought into purpose, of purpose into power.

It was one day in Switzerland that the thought of a girls' home in Philadelphia came to Bert. The two girls were at the Hotel Couthet at Chamouni. Mont Blanc was hidden by the growing darkness, and in the dimness of the room Ina threw her arm caressingly around Bert's neck, as she said, —

"I wonder, friend, how girls who are shut in and held down by what has been, and have no one to show them the may-be of life and help them to attain to it, ever get back to life and light and happiness. I wonder how many do get back, *really*. I had you, you see, and Rex. They have no one. Oh! how I pity them!"

Bert looked at her friend, and a great shining light grew in her face. Her voice was tremulous as she said solemnly, —

"Ina, my own, why should they, some of them at least, not have *me?* Why not have a place for them, a home, and a helping, in some large city where there must be so many of them? Somehow I have felt so strongly lately that God had something especial for me to do. I think he has spoken; that you are his mouthpiece."

Bert fulfilled the doctor's prophecy in part; she returned from Europe well and strong, but not as "gay as a lark." Still, always cheerful, often merry, she yet brought back a stronger mental atmosphere than she took away. An added womanliness, the impress of a great purpose, was upon her.

"Bert," said Rex, when she had been at home

a week, "you are still Bertha Hilton, but you are Bertha Hilton *plus*."

"Yes, Rex, plus a great idea," said Bert. She brought an ottoman to his feet, and leaning against his knees in the old way, spoke of her new thought and believing.

"I want to give as many unhappy girls as possible a chance," said she. "I want to secure for them home blessedness, and help them to get their piece of life sweet and wholesome and enjoyable. I haven't the plan all worked out. I want you to help me. I have a feeling that if we once open a place God will fill it with the ones he wants to come."

There was a sacrifice all around because of that talk, and what came of it, and the leading farther back. It was no slight thing to give up to the service of others one who was so much to and in her own home, but each member of the household felt that the Lord had spoken unto his handmaid, and did nothing to prevent her obeying his voice.

It was at this time that Ina became one of the Hilton household permanently. She had on her return from Europe gone with Bert to her home for a visit. She had decided not to resume her office work, as her writing now gave her a livelihood. While her plans for the future were yet unmade Bert went away, and Mrs. Hilton begged so earnestly that she might not be deprived of "*both* her girls," that Ina, feeling how much she owed to this dear family, feeling too that her lines would indeed here fall in pleasant places, stayed on, only going occasionally to Brentwood, and oftener to see Bert.

It was now three years since that house in Philadelphia was taken and made a home; a home, not with printed rules and stiff regulations, and rooms all furnished alike, but with tasteful furnishings and adornings, and homelike prettiness. Love made the rules and love kept them. When there was trouble, as there is sure to be in every large family, love was still there finding a way out of the difficulty. The house had no especial name. Homes seldom do, and this was in no sense an "institution."

By all means which love could suggest or affectionate interest devise, young girls who had been tempted and had turned aside, or were being tempted and might yield, — those who needed help from any cause, and knew not from whence it was to come, nay, rather did not expect it to come at all, — were brought into all the wholesomeness and sweetness which God had pieced together for them.

Of course the elder Hiltons and Ina were powers behind the throne, and by and by other interested ones sprang up, and the project grew into many hearts, and spread out its influences, and brought to itself and its projector warm friends and helpers.

No girl's history was known to the other girls in the house. It was enough to know that Miss Hilton loved to help the struggling, and so sought them and brought them in. Miss Hilton did not wish them to talk of each other's affairs, and her wish was law. She taught them all what consecrated friendship is, and they learned their lesson most gladly.

Bert had not chosen her work; it had chosen her, and God had anointed her as one of his ministers.

CHAPTER XXIX.

A WHOLE PIECE.

It is the will of the Lord, and his mercy endureth forever.

LONGFELLOW.

Then what matters yesterday's sorrow,
  Since I have outlived it — see!
And what matter the cares of to-morrow,
  Since you, dear, will share them with me!"

OWEN MEREDITH.

"WHY, Rex, it must be so. The whole piece has been shaping itself out of the bits and by-things. It is God's say-so. The blessedness and perfectness, the rounded-out-ness, has been preparing all these years. There is a time for coming *into* the kingdom of heaven as well as times of getting ready to go in, and when He holds the door open isn't it just as much disobedience not to enter as it is to refuse to press *towards* the door? Should we not be as ready to accept our answers to prayers as to say the prayers? If you don't heed this, and I don't help you to heed it, we are fellow sinners in common."

"But Bert, my cousin and dear girl, I have told you of my sin upon that day when you lay dying. Shall a man have such thoughts as these and pay no penance? Shall he vow a vow unto himself and his Maker, and break his promise? Shall he expect good things having done evil in the sight of heaven?"

"Rex," said Bert, her eyes luminous, her face earnest with such earnestness as only natures like hers can feel, "do you remember what Mrs. Whitney makes that delightful old Emery Ann say in 'Sights and Insights'? 'We can't help the birds flying over our heads, but we needn't let them build nests in our hair,' or something very like that. You have said you were tempted by the devil. I believe you were. But you didn't listen. The birds flew over your head; they *didn't* make nests in your hair. Why, Rex, did you ever think that if you cannot forgive yourself for having that thought, you must always blame the dear Lord for having in his mind, and longing for—for you know he was really *tempted* by these things—'the kingdoms of the world' and all the glory of them; for thinking of getting what he wanted by a short cut, which was a wrong road unto them?

Anything which is wrong in you cannot be right in him. You *have* paid penance; though I don't see as there was need, as God never wants folks to be sorry for what somebody, or some*thing*, did without their planning or consent. If you should keep the vow it is the turning your back on the kingdom, on God himself, for isn't every offered gift a part of the Father, who is love, given us in bits? He offers you what you have been, consciously or unconsciously, praying for, since you have been desiring it. If you refuse you are as far from doing his will as you would be in refusing to bear your burden patiently did he deny your prayer. Folks talk about God's will as though he never willed anything bright and glad and satisfying, and forget about the 'all things' which are as surely promised as the command to seek the kingdom is surely given."

Rex turned to the window; the very window where he had stood and prayed and been tempted. He looked straight before him into the sunlight, and again his whole heart went out to the God who answers prayer. Two sentences he repeated over and over; just a few short words, that was all. We do not multiply phrases when one or two tell all our heart's desire.

"*Lord, show me thy way. Settle this matter for me, and it shall be settled.*"

Bert left the room. She had given her word. Perhaps there would be other words, but there was something to come between them and those she had spoken. She went into the garden, picking up a kitten as she went. She sat down on a bench, and looked at the white morsel in her lap as steadily as though she was talking to it.

"More of God's happenings," she said, "my coming home just when Rex was wondering if it was right for him to keep that vow; whether it wasn't his *duty* to break it, and then thinking this might be another dire temptation. He just couldn't *help* telling me about it his heart was so full, which is another bit of the whole piece. And to come just as Ina was about to write me that she had been asked to become editor of that Western magazine, and felt as though she ought to accept the offer, as there seemed to be no farther on and *more and more* to the life here. I'm glad she thought of going, glad Rex never said he couldn't live without her. I don't believe two people are fit to stand together who cannot, if necessary, stand apart. It needs strength and endurance anyway. They can live apart, but I believe each *belongs* to the other. Haven't they grown into all the sureness and blessedness of real companionship, which makes the rest and peace of a home? Wouldn't it be like going after strange gods to turn their faces away from God's evident meanings, and seek some other outcome in life? Ina didn't understand Rex's silence. Why should she? But how sweet she was about it all when I told her! Well, Bert, it is no mean thing to be chosen as God's go-between. It all goes into the wholeness, which is the holiness, of the finished thing. He thought of you. He knew you wouldn't want to be left out. It is his always caring about even the little things which is so sweet. He knew I could give a trifle of help. He don't want the *little* pieces wasted. He told the disciples to gather up the *fragments* of the feast. He has put in your fragment, Bert Hilton."

Rex went out to find Bert, with the glory of his answered petition in his face, saying as he went,—

"I wonder if the angels whom He gives charge concerning us are always *heavenly* angels."

Ina had come into the garden, and stood by her

friend. Bert led her to meet Rex, and laid her hand in his.

"It is the gift of God," she said solemnly. "Do I love her less than in the old days when I said I should be unhappy if she loved another better than me? Better, so much better, dear Rex! But God has planned the right thing for the right time. It was best I should love her as I did then. She needed it. She was not ready for other kinds of love. She had her message to deliver before any other or a different kind came. We could have been happy had no other been ordained, but the other is here; and God has let the grandeur of loving come to me. He has taught me to love another more than myself, and to want to see the best thing come to my beloved regardless of me. I do not give her up, but hold her closer and dearer and more precious than ever before, but I acknowledge the closer claims of, and welcome, that love which shall be the crowning blessing of her life. No good thing is to be withholden. He wills it so, and He now sends her His best gift."

Great shining dark eyes were lifted to Bert's face, and Ina said, —

"Dear friend, your affection came to me as the

dawn comes after the darkness of night, and turned my mourning into joy. The noonday of love is around me, and I stand warmed and blessed and thankful in its strong rays, but I am not ungrateful for the morning love, which was so tenderly beautiful, friend of mine. Very fitting that the noon love, so strong, so sure, so steady, should follow the morning affection, and that both should be held sacred. We do not forget that blossoms were fair because we hold fruit in our hands. Very fitting that I should have a foretaste of the meridian glory through the morning softness. You gave yourself so generously, so royally! Rex, I wish you would teach me some new way of thanking our girl, for the old ways and the old words are not nearly strong enough."

Rex's hand rested lovingly on Bert's curls as he said, —

"You see, you are a large part of the 'whole piece,' little one. The web never would have taken perfect shape but for you. It has been less a weaving than an interweaving. God has held all the threads, and sent the shuttle where he would."

" Whosoever will lose his life shall find it."

Did Rex think, as he stood in that sunny garden with his heart's dearest desire granted, of the times when he had put by his soul's longings that the longings of other souls might be met in the most helpful and satisfying way? Did he remember when he stood in the empty library and offered his life for that girl-life fast going out? Did he take thought of the time when he was ready and eager to renounce all, hopes, plans, life itself, that the two loved ones might gain all?

I am sure he did not think of these things at all. He was too humbly amazed, too wondrously happy in what had befallen him, for thoughts like these to find room in his mind. This forgetfulness was a part of the losing, the putting by, which was the gaining and drawing unto himself.

The sun was going down. The summer day was dying. There came a call from the house, and the child-woman turned and went slowly along the garden path.

The night was come. Ina and Rex were together, and Bert was at peace.

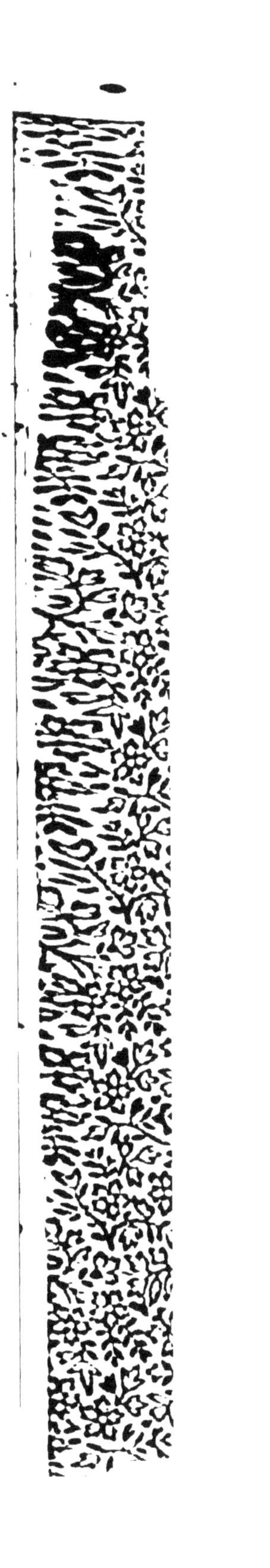

CPSIA information can be obtained
at www.ICGtesting.com
Printed in the USA
BVHW09*1333160818
524721BV00016B/1410/P